C90

A tale of two sides
by
James Josiah

The Penguins Head
26 Leigh Close
Walsall
WS4 2DU

www.thepenguinshead.com
ISBN: 978-1516989522

Copyright © James Josiah 2015

This is essentially a work of fiction, any similarities to persons living or dead is purely coincidental. Apart from Tom, he is a totally real dude and the best friend you could ever wish for. Feel free to lend this book to a friend because that's what books are for. If you want to use quotes for a review that's fine as well. Really all I'm asking is that you don't rip me off. That's not too much to ask is it?

For Sally Anne.

Without music, life would be a mistake.
  - Nietzsche

To Kay

Remember the 90s?

James Josiah

Side A - 1995

Everyone likes The Smiths.

    This is what I try to convince myself as I lie on my bedroom floor with my fingers hovering over the stop buttons of my trusty twin deck stereo. Dad calls it a ghettoblaster as if it's the eighties. I spend hours like this, trying to keep the gap between songs to an absolute minimum. This is the first track so it's easier than the rest but you still need to prepare.

    It's important to use a new tape for projects like this. I favour the C90 as 45 minutes a side is enough to flex your musical muscles but not that long that you need to go looking for longer tracks or face the possibility of losing your train of thought and using songs that have no place or purpose. The C60 is too short for most situations and you find yourself running out of time before you have even got going.

    The perfect mixtape has no filler, it flows perfectly, has songs that people know and love as well as the odd obscure track to pique their interest. It won't feature any artist more than once unless it is in exceptional circumstances or they are a guest on someone else's track.

    The obvious example here is *Under Pressure* by Queen; while David Bowie is credited you could still happily put one of his tracks on the same tape. Probably *Life on Mars...* or *Ashes to Ashes*, maybe even *Space Oddity*. It would depend on the tape in question really. I can't think of a situation that would ever call for *Dance Magic Dance*.

The inlay card isn't going to be big enough for me to write the full track listing on and my handwriting is atrocious anyway. So I'm going to try and draw something on the cover for her, even if art isn't my strong point. On the tape itself I've just written "*Becki.*"

She told me she was changing the way she spells her name in Maths yesterday. Her real name is Rebecca but everyone calls her Becky anyway so the change is purely aesthetic. I didn't tell her this of course; I smiled and said I liked it.

This is a huge step forward to where we were last year. She would talk to me and I would pretend I hadn't heard. Or reply with something totally irrelevant and make myself look stupid.

I've gone with The Smiths and *This Charming Man* as the opener. She said to Sara Jones the other day she doesn't know if she is going to go to Marion's party as she hasn't got anything to wear.

I'm not going, I haven't been invited but I wouldn't go anyway. It's hard enough spending six hours a day with the vast majority of them. Let alone pretending I don't hate them at the weekend as well.

Before I pressed record I took a pencil to the spools and wound the tape forward until the empty clear tape disappeared and the brown just started to show. There is nothing worse than a tape that cuts off the beginning of songs, especially the first one on the album; it's your one and only chance to get people's attention.

Two minutes and forty seconds after it began the song comes to an end. I press stop on both decks as quickly and as in unison as I can. I then rewind the blank tape to check the copy.

There is a second or possibly two of dead air and then the song comes crashing in, while I could probably cut the gap at the beginning down I want to get onto the next track. I fast forward through the song until I find the end, and then spend a few minutes trying to stop the tape in exactly the right point to start the next one before pressing the pause and then the record buttons.

My parents are members of a music club and every month without fail a new tape comes through the post. They don't listen to everything that arrives and are too lazy or too busy to send the ones back they don't like.

A few years back *The Stone Roses* was the record of the month, Dad gave it a go and didn't like it but from the very first play I was hooked. Normally I would have gone with *I Wanna Be Adored* and I possibly should have opened with it, but track three, *Waterfall* is the highlight of the album for me.

My ever growing collection is sorted alphabetically by artist and then subsequent albums are in release date, oldest to newest. I don't have many albums by the same artist but it's something I'm trying to address. My income is limited at the minute to the ten pounds a week I earn with my paper round. While I'm aware of how important saving for the future is I normally spend my wages on a new album from Woolworths and then depending on how much I've got left, and who is on the cover that week, a copy of NME.

I find the album, put it in the other deck and fast forward through *I Wanna Be Adored* and *She Bangs The Drums*. I listen to the end of *She Bangs* a few times, counting down to the start of *Waterfall*. Once I'm happy I've got it bang on I rest a finger on the pause button of the recording deck, hold my breath and commence the countdown in my head. The window is probably less than a second but like I say I have practiced this routine countless times and I nail it on the first attempt.

    I spend most of the four and a half minutes lay on my back day dreaming about Becki and all the possible reactions giving her the tape could bring. The best scenario I have in my head is she thanks me, goes home to listen to it and then finds me the next day to tell me how much she loves it. The worst one sees me ending up a laughing stock due to my stupid taste in music.

    There seems to be two main groups of music fans at school, the popular kids who like popular music and fawn over the likes of East 17, Ace of Base, Take That and whoever else Top of the Pops and the *Now That's What I Call Music*! albums tells them is good, and then there are the Grungers.

    The Grungers are an odd bunch. They all express their individuality by listening to the same music and dressing identically. It's all checked shirts, ripped jeans and Doc Martens. Don't get me wrong there is some alright stuff they listen to, I like Stone Temple Pilots and Pearl Jam but it's all just a bit miserable isn't it?

    The next song I want is *Castles Made Of Sand* by Hendrix, the only copy of this we own is on Dad's *Axis: Bold as Love* LP. This means I'll have to use the stereo downstairs and wait for my folks to be out so I can raid the vinyl.

    They don't have a problem with me listening to their music, in fact they actively encourage it. It's the piracy thing they have a problem with. They still believe that home taping is killing music. My take on it is if you share music with people, more people will like that artist and their sales will go up. But apparently I know nothing about the real world.

I have to wait a few days until I am home alone. I think it might be ironic that it's Saturday night and Marion's party is in full swing as I cue up the tape and drop the needle on the record, but I'm not sure. Irony is a tricky thing to get your head around.

Recording vinyl is harder than tape, you can't just skip back and forward at the push of a button. I picked *Castles Made of Sand* simply because it's my favourite Hendrix track and not enough people my age listen to him.

As I've got the place to myself I rifle through the rest of the vinyl to see if there is anything else I need to snaffle while I can. My parents have very different tastes in music. Mum spent part of her youth in Birmingham and acquired a liking for soul and Motown records, her favourite artist is Diana Ross. It doesn't even matter if she is with The Supremes or not. Dad likes rock, blues, heavy metal, basically anything with guitar solos. His favourite artist is Gary Moore.

I don't know who the copy of *Welcome to the Beautiful South* technically belongs to but I do know I love *Song for Whoever*. At a bit over six minutes long it's the longest track so far and takes me over the quarter of an hour mark, leaving me half an hour of the first side to fill. I cue the tape back up and drop the needle again, even allowing a few seconds of that beautiful crackle and pop that you only get with vinyl.

Dad is a big vinyl fan, he only ever listens to tapes in the car. He never copies his records onto blank tapes, he always buys a new version that he then keeps in the glove box. He also says he'll never buy a CD player as they are just a fad.

He also says they sound too sterile and that they are killing cover art. I don't know about any of that. All I know is tapes are cheaper and everyone owns a Walkman. I don't know anyone with a Discman.

Back in the comfort of my room I take a look at the running order so far, I realise that everything is at least a couple of years old. It doesn't stop them being brilliant songs but I want her to know that I like new stuff as well.

One of my favourite albums of last year was Terrorvision's *How to Make Friends and Influence People*. The Grungers briefly picked up on them when *Alice What's the Matter* made waves on the charts but *Middleman* is the track that has always stuck out for me.

I run through the now familiar routine of cueing the tapes and drop it in. If I'm honest I'm not really happy with its inclusion based on it being a new track alone but it's a good song in its own right.

Next up is a song I like regardless of how old it is, *Man on the Moon* by R.E.M. Dad makes out like the album is depressing but I have had to rescue it from the car on more than one occasion. I jokingly offered to do him a copy but I think I'll get him one for Christmas. *Man on the Moon's* five minute run time takes me to a quarter distance of the full album, or half way through the first side.

Once it's cued up and then committed to the tape I rewind what I have so far to the beginning and listen to it to see how it flows. The first listen was to look out for wasted time between songs, the second was focussed on the running order, the third was just because I was enjoying myself.

Sunday sees the traditional visit to my grandparents, they ask how school is going and if I have decided on what I am going to do at college yet. I tell them school is fine, because they don't want to hear the truth about how I am literally counting down the days until I leave and that the thought of college or sixth form fills me with dread.

I'd like to do something with music but I can't sing or play an instrument so that limits me somewhat. I think I'd like to be a DJ so media studies is probably a good idea, but every time I mention this to either my folks or the careers advisor at school I'm told to think of something a bit more realistic.

Monday morning and back to the grind. It rains while I'm doing my paper round so I rush it and don't get to listen to as much of Radiohead's *The Bends* as I would like. Mr Johal prefers it when I rush as people don't complain to him about their newspapers being late.

Even though it's only been out a few months I honestly think *The Bends* will go down as one of the best albums of the year. There isn't a single weak track on it, it is absolutely perfect.

The school day slides by easily enough. All anyone is talking about is the party and how drunk Steff got. Danny Connors reckons he caught her in bed with Brad Jenkins and Adam Jackson. Her public shaming and the gossip mill means people leave me alone.

We have woodwork last lesson and those who have finished them are given their plant troughs and coursework grades before we sit our exams. I haven't finished mine yet, it's still a pile of wood that needs screwing together and varnishing. Mr Smith has developed a habit of taking me to one side and telling me how important the course work is for this subject. I don't have the heart to tell him I'll hopefully never use a dovetail joint once I finally leave school.

We call him Pigeon because of the weird way he bobs his head while he talks. He knows we do it but he's one of the nicer teachers and pretends he doesn't hear it.

Becki is one of the ones who has a finished, graded product to take home. I coo and whistle and say she has done a great job on it. She says most of it was down to me and it probably was but it's her getting the B not me.

When the bell rings and the day is over she makes a fuss about trying to pick it up as if it was made out of steel and not cheap plywood. I ask her if she wants a hand. She points out that I live nowhere near her and I say its really not a problem. She says I'm a gentleman and flashes a smile that makes me blush.

It's still raining as we walk to her place and Becki insists we share her umbrella. We walk so close that our shoulders constantly bump into each other. I apologise the first few dozen times. Each time she tells me it's ok and eventually tells me to stop saying sorry.

After that I say nothing to try and avoid saying anything stupid. Becki talks relentlessly, she doesn't mention the party and I'm not brave enough to ask if she went in the end in case she tells me something I don't want to hear.

She tells me about her plans to leave town and how she wants to be a midwife. She asks what college I'm going to go to and I say I don't know. She asks about uni and I say I haven't even thought about it.

She tells me I need to start thinking otherwise I'm going to end up stuck here forever.

When we get to her place and I put the trough down on the doorstep and turn to leave. She invites me in and I say I had better be getting back before my folks send a search party out for me. She rolls her eyes, shrugs and says she'll catch me tomorrow. I smile and say *"I hope so!"* like the idiot I so clearly am.

It's gone four by the time I've walked back across town and get home. Not that it matters anyway as Dad is working lates and Mum doesn't finish until five. I find the daily note left for me by Mum with its instructions on what I need to do to start tea. It says I've got to put the oven on as soon as I get in and then put the potatoes in at four so they'll be ready for when she gets in. Tea being half an hour late isn't exactly the end of the world and I decide I'll just tell her Mr Johal asked me to help out in the shop after school. He actually does do this sometimes so it isn't an outlandish lie and far easier than the questions walking Becki home in the rain would raise.

I put the oven on and the potatoes straight in, figuring this will save me all of five minutes. I go and pick the post up off the mat by the front door and put it on the little table with the phone on. None of it is for me but there is the telltale brown cardboard package of a delivery from the music club. I don't think either of the folks ordered anything so it has to be the monthly recommendation.

It's *Above* by Mad Season, I've never heard of them or it but closer inspection tells me they are a Grunge supergroup if such a thing can exist. I know it won't be one for the folks but I have to at least give them the option of rejecting it as trash before I claim it as my own. I put it with the rest of the mail and go back to listening to *The Bends* and thinking about Becki.

I have *High and Dry* on at a bit of an obscene volume when Mum comes home. While I don't quite have Thom Yorke's range I am giving it a damn good go. She turns it down and comments on how someone is happy. I'm guessing she means me and yeah I am.

I tell her how tea is running slightly late, she tutts but says to make sure Mr Johal pays me for my time. I say I will and retreat to my room to escape further scrutiny.

Safe in my sanctuary I put *The Bends* back on and get back to thinking about Becki's tape. I rewind Radiohead back to the start of *High and Dry*, cue up the end of *Man on the Moon* on the tape and push myself ever closer to the half an hour mark. With a little over a quarter of an hour left of the first side I know I have to start upping my game.

That's another thing about a mixtape - you need to look at each side as their own beast. The end of side one may not be the end of the whole story but it is at least the end of a pivotal chapter.

After I have cued Becki's tape as close to the end of *High and Dry* as I can I scan the shelf for inspiration. While there is a lot of stuff I want to include there isn't anything that jumps out as being suitable to follow Radiohead.

As panic begins to set in that I have painted myself into a musical corner, Mum calls up that tea is ready. I hardly eat anything as I stress over the next track choice. Mum asks if I'm worried about my forthcoming exams and I tell her it's not the exams as such, it's more my woodwork coursework and that I don't think I'll get it finished in time.

This launches her off on her diatribe about how "us kids" are put under too much pressure and that I shouldn't worry as I'm never going to be a carpenter anyway. She then backtracks and asks if I want to be a carpenter before adding that manual work is nothing to be ashamed of.

I excuse myself from the table and tell her I am going to revise in my room, she tells me not to over do it, I smile and promise that I won't.

I close the door behind me and get back to the music, still at a loss with what can come next I rewind *The Bends* back to the start of side one. I probably should have mentioned this sooner but when I'm done with an album they are always rewound back to the start. I have no hard proof that leaving them half way through damages them but it's better safe than sorry.

I put *The Bends* back on the shelf next to *Pablo Honey*, a solid debut with the obvious highlight being *Creep* but just not in the same league as its follow up. Another solid debut and only a few tapes to the left is *Definitely Maybe* by Oasis, I haven't listened to it an a while and decide it'll serve as a distraction from Becki's tape.

I lie on my bed and stare at the ceiling trying not to think about anything, not the tape, Becki, school, college or my future that I am fast pissing away. I manage to get all the way to track ten before the guitar hits me like a bolt from the blue.

I'd never claim to be an Oasis fan as such because the vocals can be a bit whiney but *Slide Away* is a fantastic song, I just don't think I've ever realised it until now. I stay put until the song finishes, rewind it and listen to it again and then again just to make sure. If anything it gets better with each listen and threatens to overshadow *High and Dry*.

After the fourth listen I cue up Becki's tape and find myself under ten minutes away from the halfway point. I decide to quit while I'm ahead and call it a night. I lie in the darkness trying desperately to not think about what comes next.

School starts at quarter to nine, I live ten minutes from it and my alarm goes off at half six. Mr Johal's shop is five minutes away and my round takes me twenty minutes. There is no way these numbers add up but somehow I always find myself almost late for school. My tutor, Mrs Palmer comments every day without fail that I've made it by the skin of my teeth. My point of view is almost late doesn't really count, what's the point of being early anyway?

Tuesday runs like: this P.E, Maths, lunch and then double English. P.E sees the boys running laps of the field while the girls play hockey in the middle. With quite an absurd amount of effort I manage to stay just ahead of the main pack but behind The Dominators a small group of lads who are on all the sports teams and represent the county in their chosen fields.

Mr Roberts, a man who has taught at the school since Dad was a child and a human I can't picture in anything other than a tracksuit, told me once he was onto me. He said he just wished I'd apply myself rather than just doing enough to get by. I almost felt bad about that. He had that look about him that said he wasn't angry with me, he was just disappointed, and that's worse.

I sit next to Becki in Maths and help her with the finer points of trigonometry. I don't know how much triangles will feature in my adult life but if maths is anything to go by it's going to be a lot.

After class, Jane Ryder grabs me by the arm and asks me why I let Becki wrap me around her finger. I say I don't know what she means and she says that she'll never go out with me.

I eat lunch in what is deemed as our house's common room but is just Mrs Palmer's classroom left open for the other losers in year eleven to avoid people for an hour.

The usual crew are there, Matthew, David, Paul, Carl, who is in Kingfisher house and shouldn't really be in the Swift common room, and Gareth. The only thing any of us have in common is how desperately uncool we all are. We don't even have nicknames for each other. We don't see each other outside of school but for six hours a day we are as close to being friends as you can get without actually caring about each other.

Most of us use lunchtime to do homework that is due in that afternoon. Double English means we spend it with our noses in books trying to find hidden meanings and themes in them. Matthew, David and Gareth have *Animal Farm* and after the jokes about the mythical porno have all been made they haphazardly stumble over the concepts of communism.

Paul, Carl and myself are tackling *Romeo and Juliet*. Unfortunately English isn't broken up into skill sets like Maths so each line has to be literally broken down for the less than intelligent amongst the class.

Carl's main problem is that it isn't written in English. I can't decide if this makes it funnier that he doesn't understand when I bite my thumb at him. I'm not stupid enough to consider Becki my Juliet, after all our dads play football together so there is no quarrel between our families.

I'm not even sure if I love her, I mean you know when you love someone don't you? This is more of an infatuation that has lasted for a few years.

Becki isn't in my English class so I only get to see her for an hour today. Her set text is Macbeth. As soon as I found out I read it and made notes on it just in case she asked for help. I would offer to help but that might make her think I think she doesn't understand and the last thing I want to do is offend her.

I spend most of the afternoon doodling in the back of my exercise book while Mrs Lapin once again goes over the subtleties of teen love and suicide. I want to draw a rose on the cover of the tape. The plan being that she'll then realise it was me who left the rose and card on her doorstep on Valentine's day and not Martin Trump who took credit for them.

I walk home thinking about Jane's comment, am I wrapped around Becki's finger? Is that really a bad thing? I play the line over and over in my head, it reminds me of something but I can't quite place it.

It's Mum's day off so I don't need to start tea. Unfortunately this means it's cauliflower cheese and burgers. It's not that she is a bad cook as such it's more that she sticks to a few staples and this is one of them. I'll eat it because I'm a growing lad and I know better than to not. But mushy cauliflower in watery cheese sauce isn't my number one choice of sustenance.

It could of course be worse - it could be liver. I hate liver. I'm not that big on meat to be honest and I've thought about going veggie on more than one occasion. Dad says he'll disown me if do. I can't decide if this is a good thing or not.

The *"wrapped around her finger"* comment is still bugging me. When I go to my room after tea, I scan the shelf looking for inspiration or something to distract myself with and then the penny drops.

Linger, track seven on *Everybody Else Is Doing It, So Why Can't We?* The Cranberries debut and thus far only album. Another one of the monthly suggestions that was never returned and then eventually claimed by me. *Linger* is a beautiful, dreamy track and the inside joke aspect of it being included on the mixtape makes me giggle.

I go through the routine of cueing up the tapes and slotting it into place, by my maths this leaves me with about four minutes to finish the first side. You need to end your sides on a high, I can either do this with one brilliant track or try and squeeze two short blasts in and go for quantity over quality.

Obviously this is no real choice and I opt for the longer track, I just don't know which one yet. I let The Cranberries run their course and I get on with reading *Romeo and Juliet*.

We have been tasked with finding a quote we like that we then have to deliver to the class. I debate biting my thumb at Carl again but this would mean he would have to have it explained to him and while we might not be best friends, embarrassing him like that is a bit out of line.

I already know that most people are going to go for *"Romeo, Romeo wherefore art thou Romeo!"* This is the easiest option and the one line that everyone knows. While I might spend most of my time trying to not draw attention to myself, I like English and Mrs Lapin so this is my time to shine. I immediately decide against anything too wordy in case I fluff a line and end up looking stupid.

In the end I go for *"He jests at scars that never felt a wound"* from act two scene two. I think it means that Mercutio has never been in love so he doesn't understand the pain that Romeo is feeling. At least that is what I hope it means anyway. I practice delivering my chosen line a few times out loud until I know it off by heart and then call it a night.

I spend most of Wednesday morning thinking about *Romeo and Juliet* regardless of the lesson. Come lunchtime I chose to ditch the losers club and go looking for Mrs Lapin. She is a newly qualified teacher and we are her first class to go through the dreaded GCSE's. I find her in her classroom with her feet on her desk reading *Silence of the Lambs*. She asks me if I've ever read it and I say I haven't but I have seen the film. She gives me a disapproving look and reminds me that I'm not old enough to have seen the film legally, before laughing and telling me the book is better anyway.

She drops her feet off the table, goes back into teacher mode and asks me how she can help. I tell her my line and what I think it means. She lets my words hang in the air for a bit too long. I start to think I have got it all horribly wrong before she says how they always drum into you at uni that there will be a moment when it all clicks and you realise why you wanted to be a teacher.

Apparently I'm that moment for her, so that's nice. I thank her and apologise for interrupting her lunch. She tells me not to be silly and adds that her door is always open if I need anything. The rest of the day sort of floats by in a haze of smugness from knowing I have got something right for once.

I take a detour to the library on the way home and take out *Silence of the Lambs*. It's not that I doubt

Mrs Lapin but I just can't see anything beating the film.

Thursday starts with English and sees half the class mumble the obvious line at their shoes with no enthusiasm and I'm only really out done by Danielle Turner who has learnt Juliet's *"My bounty is as boundless as the sea."* speech from act two. I curse myself for not going for something a bit longer but clap along with the rest of the class when she finishes.

Mrs Lapin congratulates us all and says we deserve a bit of a treat and pulls a stereo like mine from under her desk. She fiddles with the volume and then presses play.

The song that follows is one I have heard before but not for a long time. You can't really call it singing but the lyrics tell a tale of a modern Romeo and his struggles in love. People look around at each other, roll their eyes and pull disgusted faces but I get it, I really do. The bell rings before the song ends and everyone except me rushes out. I sit there in silence until the end, give Mrs Lapin this awkward nod of what I hope is approval and leave.

It's science before lunch. I sit next to Becki and we quiz each other on the periodic table. With the exams so near it is like the teachers have given up on teaching us anything new and fill their days trying to remind us what we should already know.

I spend lunch reading *Silence of the Lambs* in the common room. Paul asks me why I'm reading a book when the film is already out and I tell him that everyone knows the book is better than the film.

The afternoon starts with History, a subject I have no interest in at all and only took because Becki did. Mr Samson drones on about the Cuban missile crisis and Mutually Assured Destruction as if he can bore us into learning.

The last lesson of the day is P.E. The Dominators are all on gym rotation. One of the few perks of being a year eleven is access to the weight room equipment of the leisure centre next door to the school. The rest of us end up playing basketball, no one keeps score and there isn't even really teams, we are just playing for fun and it's better for it. P.E as last lesson of the day means you can walk home in your kit, it isn't an official rule or anything it is just sort of what happens.

I run home so I can go through Dad's vinyls before Mum gets home. He has a few Dire Straits records and I go for the version on *Making Movies*. As good an album as *Money for Nothing* may be is it's a greatest hits album and thus best avoided. I play it through once with a dumb smile on my face. The second time I play it I keep a track of the run time, six minutes way too long.

Panic sets in as the entire album slips out of my control. I rummage through the records looking for something a bit upbeat, something that isn't too short or too long.

Mum has a massive collection of old soul and Motown singles, a lot of them came from the jukebox of a pub she used to work in so don't have sleeves or the normal centre hole. To play them you have to use this adapter that sits on the turntable that you then drop the record onto.

I dig and search through this treasure trove, avoiding the obviously scratched and warped and try a few of the classics out. *Stand by Me* by Ben E. King is too short, *Tears of a Clown* is too long. *Superstition* is almost perfect. I say almost as the end fades out. I hate songs that fade out, just end the bloody record already! The last few seconds are unfortunately cut off but this is what I get for over indulging earlier on the tape.

Mum comes home while I am recording it onto Becki's tape and asks what the hell I am playing at, I tell her it's a thing for school and distract her for long enough that she forgets to give me the piracy speech.

With side one potentially done I spend the rest of the evening listening to it over and over to check the flow and general feel of it. While I am happy with the flow, it is a bit rock heavy. I know The Smiths are indie and that The Stone Roses were part of the whole Madchester thing but it's all rock music really isn't it?

Genres confuse me, there are too many of them for starters, it's like people have to put everything into little boxes and make out like their contents can't be mixed or shared. I don't really believe that. Anyway what I'm trying to say is I need something a bit different to start side two off with.

Friday crawls along at a snail's pace but I get to spend half of it with Becki. First in Maths, where we have a refresher of Pythagoras just in case we ever need to find the length of any given side of a triangle but aren't allowed to measure it ourselves. And then in woodwork where my collection of parts are finally screwed and glued together and then haphazardly varnished. Pigeon asks me to stay behind at the end of the lesson and says he really should mark me down for handing it late but says that if I can get the rest of the coursework into him for Monday he'll see what he can do.

I never had any plans for the weekend bar getting on with the tape but the thought of having to spend it stuck indoors pretending to plan and design a plant pot I've already made is less than ideal.

Becki is waiting in the corridor for me when I come out, she asks what he wanted and if I'm in trouble. I almost ask her if she has ever known me to be in trouble, my entire existence is dedicated to staying out of and as far away from trouble as I can. Instead I tell her the truth.

She offers to come round and help me. The thought of having her in my room sort of switches something off in my head and I don't hear the end of her proposal.

I blink a few times to try and drag myself back to reality and ask her if she means it. She says of course she does and then asks what time she should come round. I say I have my paper round first thing. She says she isn't helping me with that and suggests after lunch, around two o'clockish. I say that that sounds perfect and she says it's a date.

I'm going to be honest. I can't decide if I imagined the smile she said that last bit with, or if she even really said it at all. Panic was sinking in about the state of my room, the house in general and how I was going to get my parents out of the way.

It's weird being in school after everyone has left, the place seems bigger, the silence imposing. It's like being in church and we almost whisper as we walk out. I walk with her through the carpark and out onto the main road. We stand in silence for what feels like ages and I want to kiss her.

I always want to kiss her, it's all I can think when I'm alone with her like this. I just wish I was braver, more attractive, more popular. I wish I was anyone other than myself. Thankfully we go our separate ways before I can build up the courage to make an awkward and probably unwanted advance.

I look back twice as we walk away from each other and each time she is looking back at me too. Each time I wave and then curse myself for being such a dork. As soon as she is out of sight I run home as if I'm being chased.

Mum comes home to find me half hidden in the cupboards under the kitchen sink where we keep all the cleaning stuff. It probably says a lot that the first thing she asks me is what I have broken. She tries not to laugh when I clamber out and tell her what I'm really doing. I had spent an hour trying to come up with some genius reason why I was cleaning my room without being prompted and wanted them out of the house tomorrow but there wasn't any plausible reason bar the truth.

I stress that it really is so I can get my woodwork coursework finished and she kisses me on top of my head and says she knows it is. She tells me to move out of the way, loads up with various bottles, cans and cloths and heads to my room.

I'm not a slob by any means but it takes us ages to make the place presentable and change the bedding. I'm then faced with an entirely different problem, it's too clean. It smells of polish and Windowlene and looks like a bedroom in a catalogue, not something someone actually lives in.

When Mum goes downstairs to get the tea on I spend as long, if not longer carefully undoing some of our work. I take books out of the bookcase and put them on my bedside table, as if I can read three books at once. I pull the duvet off the bed and then throw it back on as if I'm not going to sleep in it later but most importantly I put my stereo in the middle of my rug where it belongs.

After tea I wash up as a bit of a thank you for Mum's help and hopefully a sweetener for them doing a vanishing act tomorrow. I then go back upstairs and make a start on side two.

Keeping my rock based dilemma in mind I search for something, anything that the Grungers wouldn't like. I make it all the way to P before I find something truly suitable for a first song.

I bought the album *Dummy* after seeing the video for *Sour Times* on The Chart Show one Saturday morning. I hadn't heard anything like it before and nothing has really come close since. Dad says it's music to kill yourself to, Mum says it's a bit jazzy, but not jazzhands jazzy, whatever that means.

I repeat the process of prepping the tape by winding it forward with a pencil so the first hint of brown is showing. Slotting it into the recording deck then pressing the pause and record buttons.

Sour Times is track two and instead of whizzing through the opener *Mysterons* I let it play in its entirety. Portishead are one of the bands that demand your attention or at least they are if you want to catch every little detail they put into their work. If you are going to listen to them, I mean really listen to them, you need headphones and a decent pair at that. Dad has a good pair, so good that I'm not allowed to use them. Mine aren't bad and I saved up for weeks to pay for them but you can get better.

After the song has finished and I have checked the copy and cued the tape back up, I go back on the hunt for something non rock orientated. I don't like dance music as I don't like dancing. Not that anyone has ever asked me to dance of course, and I like my music to have lyrics. My cousin loves dance music and goes to raves, he used to copy me recordings of raves he had been to. I guess it might have been fun if you were there but it all just sounded like noise to me.

The only other thing I own that is "a bit jazzy" is Jamiroquai. *The Return of the Space Cowboy* sticks out like a sore thumb when compared to the rest of my collection. I only got it because it was in the sale and there wasn't anything else that took my fancy. It's a good album but you have to be in the right mood for it and it's not very often that I feel jazzy let alone funky.

In the end I plum for *Space Cowboy*, it's a lot longer than I remember and I'm only left with thirty five minutes of space to fill. It's hard to say I regret putting it on there as it's a nice laid back track, but time is scarce.

I decide to leave the tape for a while as anything I add at this point is going to be wrong, I can't think straight what with the lingering smell of polish and the thought of Becki being in my room. I also decide to hide the tape, I'm not expecting her to go rummaging through my stuff but a half finished tape with her name on it would be a bit hard to explain. After a few half hearted attempts where it is almost like I want her to find it, I end up stashing it in a shoebox full of photos, ticket stubs and other useless rubbish I have accumulated. I then lie on my belly and push it as far under my bed as I can reach. If she finds it there she can bloody well have it.

  To try and calm myself down I lay on my bed and try and read some more *Silence of the Lambs*. Mrs Lapin was right, it is better than the film but I start imagining Becki as Clarice and myself as Lector and that's just weird.

  I give up on reading and go back to staring at the shelf. I kid myself I'm not looking for the next track but every album that catches my eye is appraised for its suitability and then immediately rejected. In the end I grab one at random and slot it in the stereo without even looking at it. I throw myself on my bed and let myself get lost in the music.

  Andrew Knight, one of The Dominators, once said I was the type of person who would listen to Pink Floyd in the dark. It's hard to take it as the insult it was intended to be when it's true. Sometimes music just sounds better in the dark, it lets your mind take it all in and float away.

  I first got into The Cure after hearing *Friday I'm in Love*, they are consistently brilliant and if there isn't anything else that takes my fancy in the shop I always look for an album by them. My last random pick was eighty nine's *Disintegration*. Dad says they want to be an even more miserable version of Joy Division and that he didn't think much of them either. As a result I've marked Joy Division down as one of the next bands to check out. I'm just starting to nod off as *Lullaby* starts and I know I have found the next track.

My alarm clock pulls me out of a deep, dreamless sleep. I'm still dressed in my school shirt and trousers and have slept all night on top of the duvet. I don't have time for a shower before Mr Johal opens and Saturday is a bigger round than in the week so I just splash some cold water on my face, brush my teeth and rush out.

It's summertime in England, so that means it's raining. I mean what else would it be doing? I trudge round the estate as quickly as I can and am back at the shop before nine. Saturday also means pay day.

Mr Johal insists on giving me my ten pound note in a small brown envelope. I insist on opening it there and then and throwing the envelope in the bin outside. I keep telling him if he just gave me my hard earned money straight out of the till he could save himself a fortune.

Normally I head straight into town to spend my wages but that's not an option today so I run home, shower, get changed and then sit staring at the clock willing my parents to disappear and for it to be two o'clock.

Before they finally leave, Dad comes in and starts to give me *"the talk"*. He gets right to the point where a man and a woman fall in a love and the man puts his seed in the woman's belly before he cracks and starts laughing. He tells me not to do anything stupid and says they'll be back around sixish.

It's gone twelve when I realise I could of course already be working on my coursework. I find the folder I have been wilfully ignoring for at least a month and see how bad it really is. If I said it wasn't good, I'd be being generous. If I said it was disastrous, I'd be exaggerating. If I said a four hour cramming session could solve it, I'd be lying.

The task we were given is the usual preposterous proposition. The fictional Mrs Foley lives in a flat with a small balcony but misses having a garden. We are then tasked with designing and making a product that can help solve this dilemma.

The obvious answer is a reform in social housing and residential care. But Pigeon wanted us to make something out of wood not overthrow the government so we all built flower troughs.

We were supposed to carry out market research and draw up various solutions before choosing the best one. I have one drawing that sort of looks a bit like what I eventually made, my market research involved going to a garden centre one weekend while Dad looked at the fish.

We were also meant to create brainstorms, spider diagrams and flowcharts. I have a piece of A3 with *"Mrs Foley needs a flower pot"* written on it in bubble writing. I think it might be for the best if I throw that away. So while it's not good and I have less than I started with I try and crack on anyway. I know exactly what I have to do, I just can't see the point in it.

I start with product analysis. This involves drawing my trough while pretending I haven't already built it and labeling its functions. The holes I drilled in the bottom because I was bored suddenly become convenient drainage points. The rear panel that I measured incorrectly that ended up being bigger than the front is an abstract design. I don't know what to say about the feet so I just label them "feet". At a glance it looks informative and not half bad. I just hope it doesn't come under too much scrutiny.

Next up is the design specification page. Here I am meant to list every single detail I haven't thought about and then justify the decisions I haven't made. It is this I am wrestling with when the doorbell goes, my heart sinks when I realise that it is really her and this is really happening.

I try and fail at not running down the stairs and open the door flushed and out of breath. She smiles at me and I forget to invite her in and just sort of stand there staring at her. In the end she has to asks if she can come in. For some reason I decide a theatrical gesture and a bow is called for instead of saying something like *"yeah of course you can"* or something clever and funny. I close the door behind her and then show her to my room, saying on the way up the stairs that I've already made a start as if I deserve a treat or something.

I've never had a girl in my room before and despite all the work that was done last night to make it look presentable I am suddenly aware of how childlike I must come across. I have posters of bands that haven't threatened the top forty in years. Models of spaceships hang from the ceiling, I should have taken them down at least. And the centrepiece is a cheap ghettoblaster, we should have done this downstairs in the dining room.

She tosses her bag onto my bed, flops down beside it and says she has brought some stuff leftover from her project. She pulls out a seemingly neverending supply of pictures of flower pots of differing shapes and sizes. Reams of paper with sketches showing the evolution of the flower trough from its origins as a humble piece of wood. She takes a look at what I've done, grimaces and says that if I really want to pass we have our work cut out.

I feel like I have let her down so I apologise and she tells me to shut up and get to work. She tells me to start sticking the pictures onto a new sheet but to leave room so I can write about them. She says the trick is to make the page look busy, make it look like I'm excited about the project. I say I'm not that good a liar.

While I'm getting busy with the glue, she scribbles away in a notebook, giving me a steady supply of information I supposedly found out during my research. After we have the market research page done I decide it's time to play host and ask if she wants a drink or anything.

She turns down my offer of tea, coffee, wine and lager and says that squash will be fine. I run downstairs and make us drinks in the posh glasses, the ones usually reserved for guests or Christmas. When I go back into my room she is stood head cocked looking at my music collection.

This is when I realise I don't actually know what type of music Becki likes and the panic sets in that I have wasted the best part of an hour on stuff she might not like. I give her her drink and ask if she sees anything she likes. She sort of shrugs her shoulders in reply and says isn't really fussed and will listen to anything.

I tell her if she wants some music on she can pick anything she likes. She says she wouldn't know where to start and asks me what I like. My mind goes blank, I stare at the shelf and see nothing of any worth. I get all the way up to R when I see *The Bends* and ask if she has heard it yet. She says she hasn't so I put it on and fiddle with the volume until it's loud enough to be heard but not too distracting.

We don't talk while we work and the time flies by. After *The Bends* comes Terrorvision, The Smiths, Cast ,The Housemartins - anything I suggest Becki goes along with.

I can't really believe it's over when we draw up my conclusion and say how I'd like to try and take my design to market. We go over everything and both agree that while it's far from perfect it's at least something to hand in and that's more than I had a few hours ago.

I thank her from the bottom of my heart and mean every word. She asks if I want to walk her home and I say no as it's raining. She looks at me as if I'm stupid and I realise what I've said and make out like I was joking.

She tells me I don't have to if I really don't want to and I say again that I was only joking. She says that it's fine and I repeat that I was joking and make a show of pulling my trainers on. She tells me she wants to be on her own for a while and picks her bag up. I chase her down the stairs and out of the house.

By the time I step into the porch, she's already halfway down the path, umbrella up, both of us protected from the drizzle but miles apart. I tell her to wait and she turns around, I'm not one hundred percent sure but it looks like she has tears in her eyes, but maybe it's just the rain. She says that she really doesn't get me sometimes, turns and walks away.

I want to run after her but I haven't got a coat on. The idea that getting wet would somehow make it romantic flashes across my mind and I almost go. I'm not sure what stops me, it's probably because I'm a coward.

I go back into the house, close the door behind me and retreat to the safety of my room. I hadn't noticed that she was wearing perfume but the place smells of her. It feels empty without her. I know she had to leave at some point but it's like all the joy has been sucked out of the world.

I sit on my bed and try to run through everything that has just happened, to try and make sense of it. The more I go over it the more I realise I have probably made a terrible mistake.

I put my coursework in its folder, lie on my stomach and fish the box with the tape in back out. I'm going to stick to what I'm good at and make up for all this with the best mixtape I've ever made. That'll show her how much she means to me.

The tape puts me back on familiar ground and after a few minutes of finding and cueing up the start to *Lullaby* I have all but drowned out the constant stream of *"what ifs?"* going on in my head.

I decide that something cheery needs to follow The Cure and go for *Happy Hour* by The Housemartins - they are one of the few bands that everyone in the house likes. Dad prefers *Caravan of Love* and Mum takes great pleasure in reminding him that it's a cover of an old Isley Brother's song. I like *Happy Hour* because it's sort of got the pace of a punk song but it's not rubbish and it makes me smile.

I follow this up with *The Only One I know* by The Charlatans. Even though it's a few years old it's a song I find myself singing under my breath a lot. I'd never sing out loud or in front of anyone as I probably sound terrible and I couldn't cope with them watching me. They had a talent competition at school last year and as well as people entering on their own, every form group had to enter an act.

Our act was a dance routine to the then bafflingly popular song *Doop*. Everyone was involved, people played air keyboards and cavorted around having the time of their lives. I stood at the back and held a sign up, we came third. I didn't go on stage to collect our prize.

I find myself at a bit of a loss of what to put on next and end up looking towards my compilation albums. I'm never really sure where they should go in the collection, for a while I sorted them under V for Various Artists but then when I got a few of them I wasn't sure what sub-order to use after that. These days they sit at the end of the shelf in the order I bought them in. I'm still not happy with the situation but it'll do for now.

Some people look down on the compilation album and view it on the same level as a best of album. I think this is a little unfair as a compilation is a really good way to find new bands or get a certain track that wasn't on an album and if you like one track there is bound to be at least another one you'll like on there.

This is of course different to the people who only buy the *Now That's What I Call Music!* albums in the belief they are the only records you need to own. I guess it makes me a bit of a hypocrite that I own *Now That's What I Call Music 1990* but the late eighties and early nineties is where all of my favourite music comes from. There was so much going on and I wish I would have been a bit older than I am now, back then. I haven't been to a concert yet but I would have killed to have seen The Stone Roses, The Charlatans, The Happy Mondays and other bands that don't start with The.

I hate the word *The* in a band's name as people always drop it when sorting their records, it's always

Stone Roses, The. Not The Stone Roses. It's the same with solo artists Hendrix, Jimi. No one calls him that.

Yeah you can refer to him as just Hendrix but you can also just call him Jimi and people will still know how you mean. All of my solo artists are listed first name then surname - after all no one calls me Morgan, Benjamin.

The first song I pilfer from *Now That's What I Call Music 1990* is *Birdhouse In Your Soul* by They Might Be Giants. This is the perfect example of a song I didn't know I liked by a band I hadn't really heard of before being on a compilation. I keep meaning to check out more of their stuff because if *Birdhouse In Your Soul* is anything to go by they are brilliant.

The second is *This is How It Feels* by Inspiral Carpets, this is the song I bought the album for. Woolworths didn't have their debut *Life*, an album I have been after since buying *Devil Hopping* off the back of the excellent *Saturn 5* single last year. The third is buried on the second tape, I don't own anything else by Depeche Mode. I guess I probably should but I just can't see anything ever topping *Enjoy the Silence*.

The folks come home before I can add anything else to it and shout up for me to come down. They seem a bit confused and let down when I appear on my own. Mum asks if Becki is still upstairs as she'd like to meet her. I tell them she has already gone and Dad asks how I've managed to get all my work done, walked her home and managed to be back here in time for tea.

I mumble something about how I didn't walk her home and he asks if I'm joking. I tell him it was raining and he gives me that look that tells me he isn't even angry with me, he is just disappointed. I tell him she had an umbrella as if that makes it any better, all he says is *"I thought you liked her, you don't stop talking about her and you let her walk home alone?"*

He isn't even really talking to me at this point. It's as if he is trying to work it all out in his head. Mum tries changing the subject by asking if anyone wants chips for tea. Dad either doesn't hear her or decides that repeating that I let her walk home alone in a slow, deliberate and sarcastic tone is more important.

Mum tells him to leave me alone but he just needs to finally confirm that it is like they are raising an idiot in case I missed the subtleties of his previous points.

There isn't anything I can say to this so I leave them to it and head back to my room. As I'm trudging up the stairs I hear Mum say *"well what did you do that for?"*

I don't catch all of his reply but the words *"it's like he lives in a bubble!"* says everything you need to know really.

I don't own a lot of angry music and searching for something to vent my anger and frustration kind of spoils the act. I give it up as bad job and decide to wallow in my misery instead. It's far easier to wallow and I have plenty of music for it, the obvious choice being The Smiths.

Morrissey's voice lends itself to misery perfectly and while The Smiths could mope with the best of them, working on his own saw him really up his game. *Viva Hate* could be a Smiths record, it's that good, but there is just something more to it as well.

I lay on my bed and let it wash over me, Mum knocks politely on my door half way through *Everyday Is Like Sunday* and asks if I want anything from the chip shop. While I am hungry and the thought of a chip butty is tempting, I tell her I don't want anything. She asks if I'm sure and if I'm ok, I tell her I'm fine.

Before she leaves she tells me that dad doesn't mean it. I tell her he does and that he's right. I know I messed up today, I knew I was as it was happening but I couldn't stop it. Mum tells me what's done is done and to stop beating myself up about it. She reckons this is something I'll look back on and laugh about in the future, maybe even we'll laugh about it together.

I admire her optimism, I really do. But I know, deep down, that I'll never go out with Becki. At this moment in time I seriously doubt that I'll ever have a girlfriend. I ask Mum how hard it is to become a monk and if the shaved on top hair do is compulsory. She laughs and tells me girls love a funny guy. She asks me again if I want anything to eat and leaves me alone when I tell her, again, that I'm fine.

As she closes the door the intro to *Suedehead* kicks in. I lip sync along, wishing I could go and say sorry to Becki. There isn't anything really stopping me of course. I could even take the ghettoblaster and stand outside her bedroom window blasting out my apology like some soppy movie.

I rewind to the beginning of *Suedehead* and listen to it again. Girls might love a funny guy but they love grand gestures even more right? If I'm going to do this everything needs to be right. I need to finish the tape and then I'll need as many red roses as I can buy. I'm guessing you don't get many for a tenner so I'll have to wait until I get paid next week.

I rewind *Suedehead* again, pause it and then cue up Becki's tape and drop it in place. This leaves me with nine minutes left, it doesn't seem like enough to declare my undying love so I had better pick right.

Before I know it, it's Sunday again which means a visit to the grandparents and more of the usual questioning. They add a new one today *"last week isn't it?"* And yes it is the last week of school before I break up for study leave. I tell them that I leave Wednesday but that my first exam is on Friday so I only have a day to prepare for it. They laugh as if I'm joking. While I may have been in education for eleven years now I feel woefully unprepared for the next few weeks.

With three days left, school has a carnival feel to it come Monday morning. The teachers don't acknowledge this but you can see their control over us slipping away. Mr Robinson spends his last hour with us reassuring us that we know all the German we need and to not let our nerves get the better of us come the oral exam.

Science is the first time I get to see Becki since Saturday. She is already sat next to Sara Jones talking about tomorrow nights leavers ball. Obviously I'm not going. Becki asked me a few weeks back if I was going, adding that no one had asked her yet. She's going with Danny Connors now.

Mrs Gough uses her last lesson to tell us how much she has enjoyed teaching us over the years and watching us grow, she actually wells up at one point.

I realise at dinnertime that I've left my Tech coursework at home. So instead of joining my friends in the common room I run home, grab it, get something to eat and then saunter back. I'm tempted to skive off the afternoon. I've never skived off and my opportunities are fast running out. I don't of course, I've got to hand in my coursework and I've got English with Mrs Lapin. It isn't our last lesson with her but she lets us spend it revising whatever we feel we need to. I reread *Romeo and Juliet*, underlining the important bits and making notes in the margins.

Rather than looking relieved that I have finally handed in my coursework, Pigeon demands to know why I didn't find him first thing. I say it's not like he would have marked it in his lunch and he said that's exactly what he would have done. I apologise to him and actually mean it. He says he'll see what he can do but doesn't look hopeful.

Becki asks what's up when I sit down next to her and I say I'm fine. I can't bring myself to tell her that she probably wasted her time trying to help me. For the rest of the lesson, Pigeon lets us revise other subjects as his work is done. I read chunks of *Romeo and Juliet* to Becki in my best Shakespearean voice while she tries to not to laugh.

After class we walk slowly through the corridors and then the car park. At the main road I ask if she'd like me to walk her home. She smiles and says she'll be fine. I ask her if she is sure and that I really don't mind and she says again that she'll be fine. We go our separate ways and this time, each time I look back she isn't.

Dad is on earlies this week so is home when I get back and already has tea on the go. He isn't a bad cook but gets a little carried away with portion sizes. Mum always curses him saying there are starving children in Africa. He always replies that it would be cold by the time it got to them.

He asks how my day has been and I tell him there was no point going in as everything is just coasting towards the end. His reply is *"Benny it ain't over until it's over"* delivered in an ear piercingly high falsetto and so far off key it has to be deliberate. I laugh and head upstairs picking up the song where he left it.

Kravitz, Lenny, as Woolworths like to refer him as is a bit of an oddity. Most people only seem to know him for *Are You Gonna Go My Way*. Don't get me wrong it's a cracking track but *It Aint Over 'Til It's Over* is far better. I already know it's going on the tape before I've got *Mamma Said* off the shelf and into the tape deck.

Once it's on and double checked I get a little sad as I've only got five minutes left. The last track has to be truly great, everything up until this point has built to this moment. This is my last time to shine and I really need to make it count.

Five minutes is an odd length for a song, most pop records tend to weigh in around the three minute mark. Rock songs tend to lie at the six minute marker and after that you have prog. I don't get prog, no one needs that many keyboards, or a cape.

I scour the shelf mentally dismissing bands for being unsuitable for a variety of reasons. Green Day, who for some bizarre reason are wildly popular with The Grungers, rattle by at breakneck speed. Everything so far has been very laid back and kind of mellow and while it would be funny to end on such a high, *Basket Case* is barely three minutes long.

A few of The Grungers formed a band called Dog Toffee. They play all the Grunge staples with no sense of irony and sprinkle it with hits from MTV.

They played a three song set at an assembly a few months ago. *Basket Case*, *Smells Like Teen Spirit* and then *Under The Bridge*. It was part of their music GCSE and personally I would have marked them down for singing about heroin. Somehow they managed to rope in Becki, Sara Jones and Penny Lane to sing backing vocals on *Under The Bridge*, when they finished I wasn't clapping for them, I was clapping for her. The following Saturday I practically sprinted through my round and then into town so I could get *Blood Sugar Sex Magik*.

Thinking I have found my final song I dig it out and cue it up. At four and a half minutes it is ever so slightly too short. Thirty seconds doesn't sound a lot but it's a long time to listen to nothing. I could always fill it with something funny, maybe a song off one of my old Read With Mother tapes, I've still got a few lying around somewhere. Given the time and effort I've put into this I want to end it properly so I continue the search until Dad calls me down for tea.

I look at the pile of brown on my plate and ask what the hell it is. Apparently it was meant to be Toad in the Hole but we didn't have any sausages in, so he used beef burgers instead as *"they are practically the same thing."*

We eat in silence, all trying to stifle our laughter. In his defence it's not actually that bad but no one has seconds.

After tea I say I'm going to my room to revise but really I want to finish the tape. Mum, as ever, tells me not to over do it and I promise I won't. I return to scanning the shelf looking for that final glint of inspiration and come up blank.

I rewind *Blood Sugar Sex Magik*, press play and go back to reading *Romeo and Juliet*. I practically know it off by heart now but English is the only exam I really care about and the one I want to do well in.

I doubt I'll fail any of them apart from maybe technology and History but how much use are either of them in the real world? German might be a bit touch and go as the only thing I can say off the top of my head is *"Ich bin ein igel."* And I'm not even really a hedgehog.

I can understand teaching us how to order things in shops and ask for directions but why does anyone need to know what hedgehog is in any other language apart from their own? It's not like I use the word that much in my mother tongue.

I'll be ok in the main subjects - English literature and language, Maths and the sciences. I'm doing science and double science because science is just cool isn't it? Maybe I should be a scientist?

I stop thinking about school, exams and the consequences of failure when *Breaking The Girl* starts. While *Give It Away* and *Under The Bridge* where the big hits off the album, *Breaking The Girl* has always been my favourite. I close my eyes and listen, like really listen. For a few minutes it's just me and the music.

Could Becki be the girl in question? The lyrics do say they are friends and my feelings do burn for her, but I'd never want to break her. I rewind it and play it again checking the length and at a few seconds under five minutes, it's practically made to measure.

I don't really believe in fate or anything like that. My attitude towards religion is disinterested at best, but this feels right. I would never have chosen the song, especially as the closer but it's like it has chosen itself.

I cue the tapes up for the final time and five minutes later it's done. I don't know how many hours I have put into it. And while I haven't even drawn the cover yet I think it's been worth it. I just hope she likes it.

I spend the rest of the evening listening to it and practicing drawing roses for the cover. Some of them I colour in, others I try shading. All of them look crap. Dad is handy with a pencil and I could always ask him, but it feels like cheating. This has been all my own work so far and it would be a shame to spoil that so close to the end.

When the tape clunks to the end of the second side I take it out of the deck and put it into its case. I turn it over in my hands a few times and practice things to say when I give it her. Each line I come up with sounds awkward and stupid or forced and wooden - maybe I should just leave it on her doorstep or try and slip it into her blazer pocket?

Mum knocks on my door to let me know it's eleven o'clock. It's not that it's my bed time or anything like that but she doesn't want me staying up all night when I have school in the morning.

I lie in the dark and try not think about Becki hating the tape and laughing at me for making it. Dad says being a pessimist means no one can ever let you down. Mum says being optimistic means you see the best in everyone. I don't know where I fall. I try to be positive but it's just hard at times you know?

It's Tuesday and my last full day at school starts with P.E. Mr Roberts tells us we can do what we want as long as no one gets hurt. The Dominators hit the gym and everyone else ends up playing murderball.

Mr Roberts joins in and hits Carl on the back of the head with a tennis ball.

Maths is my last lesson with Becki. I don't mention it as I'm trying to be aloof and cool. She spends the entire lesson talking to Sara about tonight's ball and how Danny is going to pick her up in his dad's Mercedes.

Dinnertime sees Carl moaning about how he has a lump on the back of his head and how he could sue the school. There is no mention about how this is the last time we'll probably all be together and no plans are made to meet up in the summer. It is like we all know when we walk out tomorrow that'll be it for us.

Double English in the afternoon restores a sense of normality as Mrs Lapin is determined to teach us as much as she can in what little time she has left. I walk home in a daze, my mind full of verbs, nouns, pronouns and similes.

The evening vanishes away from me. The folks don't mention the ball and how I'm not there but it's kind of deliberately not mentioning it and they end up drawing more attention to it. I don't even know if I could have brought myself to ask Becki, let alone what I'd have done if she would have said yes.

In my room I commit a crude drawing of a rose to the cover of her tape. I don't colour it in or try and bring some detail to it by shading. It is literally just the outline and could be any flower in the world but it is recognisable as a flower so I guess that's one thing. I put the completed tape in my blazer pocket ready for tomorrow. I've decided I'm just going to walk up and give it her. I'm not going to say anything on the basis that I won't end up saying something stupid.

My nerves bubble up inside as I try to sleep. I don't know if it's because of the tape or the mixture of excitement and relief of school finally being over. It's gone midnight before I finally drop off and I am awake before the alarm goes off.

For as long as I can remember year eleven have always been contained on their last day. Legend has it that it's to stop us setting off the fire alarms or causing trouble with the lower years. Personally I think it's to stop us rubbing their faces in it.

The day starts with a final assembly that is meant to be jovial. Comedy awards are given out. I've been shortlisted "Least Likely To Leave Town" and my cheeks burn scarlet as I'm forced to stand up and accept my round of applause. Becki wins "Most Likely To Leave Town" and is given an A-Z of London.

I try to catch Becki afterwards but she is swept away in the crowd as we all return to our form groups. Our tutors have all of our coursework from various subjects and other useless trash that we don't need but have to take home.

Pigeon, God bless him, has somehow managed to grade my project as a D. The coursework makes up sixty percent of the final grade so I'll have to really go some to tank technology.

And then two hours later, after we filed in for the last time, we are sent on our way. I loiter at the edge of the car park waiting for Becki. Passing the tape from hand to hand, trying to find some way to hold it and look casual. A few people say bye to me and some of them even manage to sound like they mean it.

My heart sinks when I finally see her walking arm in arm with Danny. She has her head leant into him and he has a smug look plastered all over his stupid face. She smiles when she sees me and waves and I wave back like the idiot I am.

They are out of earshot so I don't hear what Danny says to her before he appears to try and shove all of his tongue down her throat. I put the tape back in my blazer pocket and run home.

Side B - 1999

Tuesday.

Tuesday means the big delivery. It means Kerrang! comes out tomorrow. It means two days until the funeral. Three more until the weekend and I'm not doing overtime Saturday morning no matter what Daryl says. It means a week until the gig.

I figured out a while back that the secret to getting through life is breaking it down so you always have something to work towards. It used to be that I counted down until the next drink. We used to go for a pint in the White Lion everyday. It got to the point that the drinks were ready for us on the side when we got there. Then it was a pint and a half, then two.

I don't drink anymore. I'm an all or nothing type of guy these days and it was getting out of hand. I'm not, nor was I ever, an alcoholic, I just prefer being drunk to being sober. I prefer being asleep to being awake but I'm not a sleepaholic.

The radio is back on so that means it's 15:30 and another hour until I'm out of this dump. Since the merger a few months back, we have too many staff to have the radio on all day and the management are far too cheap to pay for a broadcast licence. So what happens is we get hour long slices of Radio 1 followed by soul crushing silence.

I tried working with my Walkman on a few times. Each time I was caught and had it taken off me. The last time, Daryl said if he caught me with it again he'd smash it. The place is worse than school, it's like prison without the privileges.

I went to the union about it and they said I should really be a member but that using the Walkman was a health and safety breach. They wanted to know what would happen if the fire alarm went off and I didn't hear it? I pointed out that Bobby is deaf and he hasn't burnt to death yet and they told me to not to be pedantic.

I'm meant to be putting away this new line of tailored shorts. They are fairly hideous but I reckon if I got a pair a few sizes up they'd be alright to skate in.

Pistol Pete, the security guard will be around in a minute, on his last round of the day. He'll then go and stand by the exit and watch us all clock out before deciding to do a random bag check on one of the girls. I doubt Pete even realises you could set your watch by him. It's not that he's thick or anything, well he is but that's not the point. This place is nothing but routine and it's more that I'm smarter and more cunning than he could ever imagine.

What I'll do is wait for him to go by, take the pair I want down into the fire escape, slip my camo trousers off, put the shorts on and then put my trousers back on over the top. It's so easy it's almost boring stealing from here. It's not like I really need them either, I went through a phase where I was having two pairs away a day. One at dinnertime, one at hometime. It got to the point I couldn't even give them away. I'm not saying I wanted to be caught but really getting the sack wouldn't be the end of the world.

I'll have been here two whole years come the end of the month. I wonder how many pairs of cheaply made trousers I will have unpacked by then? Too many is the only acceptable answer to that question.

They are all made in the same factory in some eastern bloc shit hole. One of the small pleasures in my life is that the staff over there will be getting paid even less than I do. They are then bagged up into bundles by the Romanian version of me. Loaded onto a lorry and transported across the continent to here.

They are then unloaded by the loaders. Unbagged by me and Paul. Counted by Darren. Steamed by the girls, then taken into storage by me and Paul. They'll then sit in storage for anywhere up to a few weeks before they are picked by Justin and Phil, packed back up by the packers and sent across the country where they are sold for a scandalous amount of profit in various stores.

I can never decide if it is ironic that I couldn't actually afford to buy them in the shops. Irony is a tricky thing to get your head around.

Shorts successfully stolen and security avoided, I head home. I passed my driving test a while back now and am the proud owner of an F reg, sky blue Ford Fiesta. Proud is probably a bit of an exaggeration, it's a hunk of junk. Despite holding down a full time job and still living at home, I struggled to save up for a car and ended up taking a loan out.

Luckily the bank were more than happy to throw money at me. I only wanted a thousand pounds to get me on the road. I walked out with five thousand pounds and a credit card. They did offer me as much as ten thousand pound and the thought of buying something stupid like a Ferrari did cross my mind, but the insurance would have crippled me.

In the end the car cost me five hundred pound, insurance and tax took another five hundred pound. The rest of the money I've spent on a new stereo, clothes, a skateboard, hundreds of CDs, gig tickets and other essentials. Really it's a good job I don't drink anymore as I would have probably wasted it.

The stereo is my pride and joy. It's got a three disc changer, twin tape decks with auto reverse and one hundred and fifty watt speakers. I've only had it at full blast a handful of times, each time to show people just how loud it could go. If I didn't still live with my mum, or had the neighbours to worry about. Once I have my own place it'll be on full blast all the time.

The drive home takes about five minutes. I know it doesn't really do the car any good and that I should walk. But driving means I can stay in bed for an extra twenty minutes in the morning. It's not that I'm lazy or anything I just find the world to be a more enjoyable place with the curtains and my door closed.

Mum asks me if I'll be dining in tonight, I tell her I had a big lunch and will grab something later. I didn't and I won't but she doesn't need to know that. I don't really eat all that much of late. It's kind of hard to explain why but it's one of the few things in my life I have utter control over. I turned vegetarian when I stopped drinking, I even ditched caffeine as well. It's all part of the whole Straight Edge vibe I've got going on.

Straight Edge is this massive scene in America, not so big over here. Especially in this dead end town I'm trapped in. There is no real culture here, unless you count excessive drinking, casual violence and being an Oasis fan.

I tried explaining it all to Mum. I didn't give her the real reason I had decided to clean my act up of course, no one knows about that. She never said as much but I think she is just glad I'm off "the drugs" these days.

If we are being honest I was never even really on drugs. I smoked a bit of pot now and then. I took acid once and spent the entire trip marvelling at how long my arms were. And then there was the mushrooms. The last time I took them I had an out of body experience and thought I had died. Mushrooms are like a rite of passage round here. They are free, 100% natural and grow in abundance, really it would be wrong not to try them at least once.

I've never done speed, ecstasy or cocaine, they are all on the wrong end of the spectrum for me. I like to be relaxed, chilled, numb, detached from the world. Heroin is making its mark around town, and I have gone out of my way to avoid it. While the end result would be what I'm after, being a junkie just isn't a good look is it?

There are rumours going round that Jon, a kid who was in my year at school has been reduced to sucking off lorry drivers for a few quid to get his next hit. The dude isn't even gay.

The gig is a week away so we need to start making preparations for the road trip. A new tape is called for I reckon. While I've thought about putting a new stereo in the car it would essentially be a waste of money. A decent one would probably double the value of it for starters. Then I'd have to get new speakers for it as well and I haven't got that type of money to throw around anymore.

I pull a box out from under my bed, rummage around in it and eventually find what I'm looking for. It takes about an hour and a half to drive to Wolverhampton so a C90 is exactly what we need. The case is scratched and the cover has a picture of what I think was meant to be a rose crudely drawn on it. The box is full of tapes; the majority of it is what I used to laughingly yet lovingly refer to as the collection.

I take the tape out of its case, screw the cover up and throw it in the bin. I try to peel the sticker off so the word *"Becki"*, written in my childlike scrawl, is no longer visible. It doesn't work so I scribble over it with a marker pen stolen from work, obliterating the past. The tape deck of the new stereo, opens silently and I slot the tape in.

I press play and the jangly intro of *This Charming Man* fills the room. Sadness and regret seep into my very being. I remember lying on the floor in my room utterly convinced that 90 minutes of crappy indie tunes would somehow make her love me. Even after all this time I still think I might love her, I still fantasise about how she is the one.

Becky works at the factory these days, in the offices mind, she is far too smart to work out on the floor with the likes of me. Her dreams of the future and escape were dashed when she met a boy at college, fell in love and tried to settle down. He left her for some skank he met in the club and hasn't been seen since.

Her not leaving town feels wrong, criminal almost. We all knew I was never going to be going anywhere, but she was meant to be different. It's like we are all trapped here, all destined to make the same mistakes our parents made and their parents before them. Sometimes I think the place must have been founded on misery and failure. We still speak when we see each other, it's just our paths don't really cross anymore.

She was the one who told me he had died. I was working down the back aisles, putting an order of blue cords away that were destined for old men up and down the country. She tapped me on the shoulder and didn't say a word when I asked her what was wrong. She started crying so I awkwardly hugged her and then she just sort of blurted it out.

Not really feeling up for a trip down memory lane I turn The Smiths off, then rewind the tape and press record, replacing the sounds of my youth with crisp, fresh, new silence.

I know I should probably wait for Tom but I want to get started, after all we haven't got long and this needs to be utterly perfect. I start with *Pigwalk* by Stuck Mojo, it's a cracking track but wouldn't really work anywhere else on the tape due to the intro.

I rewind the tape, take it out of the deck and wind the spools forward using a pencil until the brown is just starting to show. I then put it back in the deck, press pause and then record. Tape ready it's time for the disc.

Cueing up a CD is far easier than tape. It's just a case of putting the tape in, finding the track, pausing it and then skipping back to the start. It's almost too easy. Not that I could ever afford one but you can make playlists on a computer and then copy it to CD. No cueing up, no fretting on the run time. No skill or talent required. I know the mixtape is slowly dying but I don't want to imagine a world where they no longer exist. They do say ignorance is bliss.

Please Sir by Pitchshifter comes after *Pigwalk*. This is the first Pitchshifter track but it won't be the last. Normal rules of only having one track per band are going to be tossed aside as this is being made especially for the gig.

The album *www.pitchshifter.com* came out last year and has been a favourite ever since. I've even worked backwards and bought their earlier and much heavier stuff. *Please Sir* is a few seconds shorter than *Pigwalk* and matches it for pace and aggression. This tape is going to be full throttle, balls out, from start to finish. I want to arrive at Wolverhampton ready to tear the place a new arsehole.

I spend a lot of my time angry or frustrated these days and the music reflects this. It's all pounding drums, crunchy guitars and angry young men. I thought for a while that maybe the music was steering my mood so I tried listening to some more upbeat stuff. It sort of worked as well. I mean you just can't listen to A or Symposium and be pissed off with the world.

It just wasn't enough, the rage was still there. I just wasn't channelling it anymore. It built and built and built, my contempt for everything grew toxic. The suffering around the globe and people's indifference to it ate away at me like cancer. People are dying in their thousands in Kosovo and the people I work with are more concerned with how United are going to do in the league. They make me sick.

I stopped watching the news and reading the papers in the end. It was all getting too much. I wasn't sleeping properly and I stopped eating all together for a while. I thought about going to the doctor's but I didn't know what I would say or what could even be done about it all. I mean how many other nineteen year olds are worried about Ebola? I don't want to end up on the happy pills or in the nuthouse, so I ignore it in the hope it'll all go away.

My self treatment of heavy metal and blissful ignorance works wonders for the most part. There is only the occasional day where I think about going in to work armed to the teeth and slaughtering all who stand before me.

Most of the people at work wouldn't even see it coming. They seem to think I exist just for their amusement. They see the army surplus clothes, the band t-shirts, the hair hanging in my eyes and write me off as some type of idiot.

Tom rocks up as I'm cueing up *Good God* by Korn and I fill him in on the plan to make the mixtape to end all mixtapes. He is of course immediately on board and starts looking for the next track.

Tom is pretty much my only friend these days. I've burnt a lot of bridges with some pretty dumb behaviour but he has stuck by me. He's a few years younger than me and some people think that's a bit weird but we're just on the same level.

We met pretty much by accident a couple of years ago. It was the summer holidays, the school had been given some lottery grant and installed six basketball rings on the tennis courts. While I may have spent most of my life trying to escape school, I love basketball. I was there with Carl, Tom was there with Huw. We played a few games of two on two and by the end of the day we were friends. By the end of the holidays we were all inseparable.

It was the music that brought me and Tom together, Carl and Huw were more about the game and played every chance they got. We slowly drifted apart into two new groups over the winter months as less ball was played and more hours were spent in my dingy room.

I know he should really be revising for his exams but I kind of respect our time together as being totally away from all of that for him. It's weird to think he is in the same boat I was in 95 but I know he won't mess it all up like I did. He has it all figured out, college then uni. No messing about. He knows what he wants out of this life and he's going to grab it.

He follows up *Good God* with *Know* by System of a Down. I kick myself for not picking it sooner even though it is only track four. *Know* is the sort of thing our band, Summer Holocaust, will play once we have a full line up. So far it's just the two of us, Tom on guitar and me on vocals.

Tom is an amazingly good guitarist, he has lessons every Saturday morning. I've bought an amp and a microphone that set me back almost as much as the car did. I've thought about getting singing lessons so I can at least carry a tune when needs be. But really how hard can shouting be?

We sort of have one song already, *Puny Banner*, it's a chugging sort of punk riff and has the chorus of *"HULK CRASH! HULK BASH! HULK SMASH!"* that I'll deliver in the monosyllabic fashion of the big green beast.

Whilst it might not be heavy, *Powertrip* by Monster Magnet is a magnificent tune and perfect for a roadtrip. The first time I heard them was when *Dead Christmas* was on a tape that came free with Kerrang! a while back. I had all but forgotten about them until they were the support for Rob Zombie last year.

The Rob Zombie gig was the first time I drove to Wolverhampton having passed my driving test a few weeks before. I still have no idea how we would have got there if I had failed. It was a Monday and I took the day off work so we could leave in plenty of time to get there. We left in the middle of the afternoon, sailed all the way there and found ourselves with hours to kill before the doors opened.

The gig itself was a bit odd, it wasn't that Mr Zombie was bad it was more that Monster Magnet were just better. I've never been one for theatrics in music. I'll take long hair and sunglasses over face paints and costume changes every day of the week. Saying that Kilgore did the same to Fear Factory a few days later, our second trip to Wolverhampton in less than a week. Maybe it was just a bad week for headliners?

We follow Monster Magnet with *T-1000* by Fear Factory, it's a DJ Dano remix of *H-K* and a bit of a joke between us. We don't listen to anything that wouldn't appear in Kerrang! That's really the best way to describe our music taste. *T-1000* with its thunderous beats is the only way we'll listen to anything that could be described as dance music.

We're about due some more Pitchshifter and we go for *Underachiever* off 96's *Infotainment?* album. If I was being pedantic I would point out that when they released *Infotainment?* the band were known as Pitch Shifter rather than Pitchshifter, but I'm not so I won't. I just hope they play it. Writing a set list has got to be tricky. As an artist you're going to want to air your newest masterpieces but the crowd never wants to hear new stuff, they want the hits they can sing along to.

When Pitchshifter comes to an end we decide to go out and get some fresh air. It's just getting dark as we cruise the streets in the Fiesta like some sort of rusty shark. We do the figure of eight loop through town a few times and don't see anyone of any interest.

Like a rock thrown into a pool, his death is sending ever increasing ripples out there. I'd never count myself as a boy racer anyway. I mean it's hard to be taken seriously when your car has a one litre engine and its bodywork is mostly made of rust but the police take an interest in us as we make our fifth loop of the evening. It's not the first time I have been pulled over and it won't be the last. They just ask what we are up to and tell us to be careful, it's not like we are breaking any law and I don't blame them at all. This is a small town and the general consensus is that if they had done something about him earlier he would still be alive. It's not their fault he is dead of course, it was an accident and that's what messes me up the most.

We were the same age, I think that's what hit me the hardest. You tend to think you're immortal at this age don't you? Everything is always going to happen to someone else. I mean I know I'm going to die at some point, we all are, but him just dying like this has made life seem so fragile.

We weren't friends at school. We weren't enemies either, he always left me alone. If anything, I doubt I even appeared on his radar. It was at college that we got to know each other properly. I'm still not sure how we ended up on the same course. Maybe his grades were as bad as mine and it was that or nothing. I was somehow cooler for knowing him and he never told anyone on our course that I was a loser.

He was the first out of us all to pass his driving test, the first to get a car. He used to give us lifts to and from college and take delight in seeing how fast he could go down the country lanes, seeing if he could make any of us tell him to slow down. I never did of course, I never said anything. I was terrified that I would be cast aside at any moment so I laughed along with him and urged him to go even faster.

It wasn't a shock when Becky came and told me what had happened. I hadn't really seen him since I dropped out of college but I had heard the tales. Everyone in town knew his name and what car he drove. It still knocked me for six. It wasn't a shock but he didn't deserve it, he had his entire life ahead of him.

Tom says the school is holding a minute's silence for him on Thursday. I say it's a nice gesture even if most of the kids won't have a clue who he was. I asked for the day off work to go but was told I'd have to book it as holiday as he wasn't anyone close to me. I didn't think they were going to give me it all but I pretty much told Daryl I'd ring in sick if I had to.

We call it a night and I drop Tom off at his place before heading back to mine. Mum is already in bed when I get in. She says I treat the place like a hotel I say it is a pretty shitty hotel as it doesn't even have a pool. She keeps saying she's going to kick me out if I don't buck my ideas up, whatever that means.

Wednesday, halfway towards the weekend. This time next week Pitchshifter will be done and dusted and the countdown to Fugazi will begin. Fugazi are one of the reasons I went Straight Edge in the first place. Their last album *End Hits* is a bit different to what I was expecting but I'm still holding out they play some Minor Threat stuff.

I grab Kerrang! on the way to work. Reef are on the cover - a vast improvement over Cradle of Filth last week. There is a small piece about the Pitchshifter gig, the first 100 people will get a goody bag. I have no idea what'll be in it but I want one.

Becky comes to find me before lunch to make sure I'm still going tomorrow. I say I'd really rather not go and she says she knows what I mean. She asks if I'd mind if she came with me. I ask what time she wants picking up, then start rambling in the excitement of being with her. I tell her the service is at 11:00 and it's going to be packed. Then I say how I heard they are putting speakers outside, before adding that if we want to get good seats we'll have to get there early.

As I hear the words "good seats" come out of my mouth I know they aren't the ones I want and I immediately start to back track. She tells me to shut up, says she knows what I mean and to be at her place at about half ten.

The rest of the day pretty much just floats by as I daydream about our date. I know it's not really a date but it's as close as I've gotten to one in a long while. I'm not a stranger to the way of a woman but put it this way, I hope it really is like riding a bike. Not that I'm calling Becky a bike of course.

After skipping tea and making sure my shirt still fits, I ask Mum if Dad left a black tie behind when he left. He's been gone about six months now but his presence lingers heavy over moments like this. Mum says she doesn't think so and that I've left it too late to get one now. I can't go to a funeral and not wear black, I'd look like some type of idiot. It's bad enough I don't own a suit and will be wearing trousers I've stolen from work paired with my scruffy Doc Martens. I've tried to polish them up but the scuffs I worked so hard to get, to really perfect that *"I don't care about anything"* look just aren't shifting.

Mum suggests asking Steve next door if I can borrow his. I tell her not to worry about it and say I'll go into town and buy one first thing, least I'll always have one then. This will be the third funeral I've gone to and the second one of someone my age.

The first one I went to was my Grandad's. I was twelve and it really messed me up. He had suffered with cancer for a long while and was just a shadow of the man he was when he died. I refuse to call it a battle or a fight, you can't fight cancer any more than you can push water upstream.

I wasn't sad when he died, it meant he wasn't in pain anymore, and I felt guilty about that. They cremated him and when the curtain closed around the coffin, that was when it really hit me that I wouldn't see him again. In the six years since I've only been to his grave once. I don't need to look at a stone with his name on or put flowers down to remember him, I'll never forget him. He was the greatest man I'll ever know.

The second was a few years later and for a girl who lived across the road. Her death shocked everyone. She was super popular, clever and had the perfect family. Then one day she went home from school and hanged herself. I still can't get my head around it. On nights when I can't sleep and the bad thoughts come creeping in, I hear her mother's screams from when she found out.

I ended up seeing a counsellor for a while after she died. Mum talked me into it as it was obvious I wasn't coping. I felt guilty about that as well. Who was I to struggle with her death? Her folks had lost their child, I'd only lost someone who I played with after school and in the holidays. I stopped the counselling when I ran out of things to say, there was stuff I never admitted to them but we all have our secrets don't we?

Tom comes round before I've changed back into the uniform of the greebo. Pretty much everything we wear these days is either black, army surplus or both. Chains hang from our hips - they are meant to keep wallets secure but mine used to be attached to a bottle opener. This was after I cracked my teeth opening bottles but I still wanted to be able to always have a drink if I needed it.

He asks how my day has been and I tell him to never get a job in a factory. He laughs but I tell him I'm serious. It's too late for me. I've made my bed and now I've got to lie in it but he can be different. He still thinks I'm joking so I change the subject and tell him about how I'm going to the funeral with Becky. I also tell him about how I need to buy a tie in the morning and he suggests going to Pitchshifter in white shirts and black ties. It's a look that their guitarist Jim Davies has rocked a lot and a brilliant idea. We talk about the possible contents of the goody bag that we are both absolutely positive that we'll be getting and crack on with making the tape.

We start the evening with *Steamroller* by Kilgore. Kilgore are the best band I've ever seen. They opened for Fear Factory last year and wiped the floor with them. I bought their album *A Search For Reason* off the bass player at the merch stand and told him so as well. It's such a great record, it's more than just another metal album. A lot of this is down to Jay Berndt's vocals, the raw emotion he puts into *Providence* makes me come out in goosebumps. It's hard to describe just how much music, and songs like *Providence* mean to me. It's like these people who don't even know I exist, understand all the messed up shit in my head that I can't tell anyone.

While *Providence* might keep my demons away, *Steamroller* is an altogether different beast. It's the first song on the album and grabs you by the balls. It doesn't let go until it comes crashing to an end a little over two minutes later. We follow *Steamroller* up with

Like This With The Devil by Entombed. While they might not be the type of band we normally listen to, they impressed us when we saw them at Ozzfest last year.

Pantera are another band we saw at Ozzfest. For some reason I still don't really understand we were in the queue to meet Soulfly when Pantera took to the stage. We stayed there right up until they started playing *Walk*. It was like the band were beckoning us and we abandoned our spot in the queue and charged into the thick of it.

While they were great I have less happy memories of their set than I do of Entombed's. While they have really clamped down on crowdsurfing at gigs, it is still tolerated at festivals. It's not like they were going to kick you out and we had pretty much done it all day. We look at it as a sign of appreciation, a means of escape or a way to get closer to the band. Either way I was on top of the crowd, the band were doing their thing and then someone punched me square in the balls.

I try to be a considerate crowdsurfer. I never wear boots to gigs and don't kick out at the people below me. I don't know if this fella had been having a bad day, if he had been clobbered earlier or if he thought I was someone else. What I'm saying is there has to be a reason why you choose to punch a total stranger in the nuts, doesn't there?

I know it wasn't the band's fault but that's all I really took away from their set and all I ever think about whenever I hear them. In hindsight I'd much rather have waited and met Max Cavalera. I still don't try and talk Tom out of putting *A New Level* on the tape as it's a cracking tune even if it does elicit a Pavlovian reaction in my groin.

We are fast approaching the end of side one and the usual rules apply so we need to up our game. First up is *Davidian* by Machine Head, your classic metal band. They have been on the scene for years now and their third album is out in a few months. For some reason we haven't seen them yet, but I'm sure that'll change when they tour next time.

Next up are a band we have seen, Deftones. Their second album *Around the Fur* has the sexiest guitar sound I've ever heard but we ignore that for now and go with their debut album *Adrenaline* and *7 Words*. And then that leaves us with a little under four minutes to fill. My first thought is *Triad* by Pitchshifter but it's about a minute too long so we go with *Virus* instead.

With half of the tape done we decide to go out and give it a blast. 45 minutes is too long to kill looping around town so we head out into the countryside. I thought I was driving aimlessly but we soon found ourselves where it happened.

There is still police tape fluttering in the breeze, the flowers left in tribute are starting to rot. I try not to think about what that must mean about him. The skid marks are still as bold as the night they were laid. They start on the apex of the corner on the right side of the road and then carry on defiantly onto the opposite side until they meet the kerb. There is then churned grass, mud and a gaping hole in the hedge. The car is long gone but there are still bits of glass and plastic lenses that shimmer in the dying sunlight.

There were four of them in the car, heading back into town after a car meet. I'm not saying they were racing. Everyone involved said they weren't racing, but CCTV shows them leaving the meet in a hell of a hurry. There was no dramatic fireball, the three passengers all walked away without a scratch on them. They say he died instantly, that he wouldn't have felt a thing. As if that makes it alright. His last moments on this earth, no matter how fleeting would have been of fear, panic and that sinking feeling you get when you know you have fucked up.

I wasn't there that night, like I say I'm no boy racer and the Fiesta wouldn't exactly fit in at the meets. They don't hold them anymore. They weren't officially cancelled or anything, people just stopped turning up. I wasn't there but I still feel guilty, I'm not sure what I could have done if I was. But I wasn't so the world of what ifs and maybes haunt me.

Tom hasn't seen it before, I normally come out here alone. I haven't left flowers. I don't see the point and I'm definitely not going to be leaving a can of cider for him. He wasn't drunk, that rumour was quickly shot down. It was just an accident, a tragic life wasting accident.

Wary of being caught there the night before the funeral blasting heavy metal, I turn us around and head back into town. Tom doesn't mention how slow I'm driving and brings the music back as the focus of our attention. What we have is good, it flows nicely and every tune is a belter. But it could be heavier, it needs to be heavier.

Even though it's not even nine o'clock I drive Tom home and say I'll probably catch him Friday. He tells me to not do anything stupid tomorrow and I promise him I'll be alright. He's a smart kid that one, he knows I'll mess up long before I ever do and always tries to stop it happening.

Mum is still up when I get home, seeing her more than once a day is a rare occurrence lately. She asks if I'm ok and tells me tomorrow will be hard but to not let it get to me. I tell her I'll be fine and that I'm going with Becky. It's still early but I say I'm going to go to bed as I want to be fresh for it all.

Apart from just generally being drunk, one of the things I miss the most about drinking is being able to go to sleep. Being a drunk is like being able to fast forward your life, one minute you're being asked to leave a party and then BAM! It's the next morning and you're safe and sound in your bed. Sure sometimes your bed is a bench in the park or the backseat of your car or maybe even a hospital bed. But you have no idea how you got there so it's ok.

That's what I think about as I lie staring at the ceiling willing, daring sleep to come. It doesn't, well not in a hurry anyway and by 03:00 I have pretty much run over every stupid little thing that has ever happened in my life in great detail. I start with the sports day in infants school where I fell over in the obstacle race and cried until Mum had to come and pick me up. Then there is the time I tripped over a loose paving slab outside the junior school entrance and broke my wrist. I lay there and cried until I was picked up that time as well. Then there is senior school and all the stupid things I said and the wealth of things I was never brave enough to say.

I wasn't really at college long enough to make a show of myself. The biggest regret there is dropping out. Well that's not strictly true the biggest regret there is not signing up for a course I was actually interested in. Catering and Hospitality was what I ended up with. The only one in the prospectus that vaguely interested me and would accept me based on my grades.

2 C's, 4 D's, an E and an F. That was what I managed to walk away with. The C's were in English and a grade below what I was expected to get. The D's were in German, maths, science and double science. The E was in technology and I still feel like I should track Pigeon Smith down and apologise for that. The trough is still by the front door and has pansies in. F was in history and I feel like Mr Samson should find me and apologise. As much as I didn't want to be there and he didn't want to teach us, he still taught us the wrong syllabus. A few parents did actually complain about him and he is rumoured to have been offered early retirement. Some of my class even did re-sits, so I guess it's true that if you don't learn from history you are doomed to repeat it.

I don't know just how late it was when I finally dropped off but Mum knocks on my door at 09:00 and tells me I'll need to get a move on if I want to get ready and get into town to buy a tie before meeting Becky.

Even though I don't really need to I have a shave, trying and failing to not cut myself in the process. I quite fancy growing a beard, not a poncey goatee, a proper beard like a viking would have. Growing a beard can't be that hard, I mean it requires no effort at all. It's actually harder to not have one. I can go weeks without shaving as it is and nobody notices so I guess that'll have to wait until I'm older.

Puberty was an odd experience, I think I am what people would call a late bloomer. I mean I have pubes, that was never a problem, but I still look a bit like a kid. I'm old enough to drive, vote, drink and have sex. But when I look in the mirror I still see the me I've always seen.

I thought life would change when I turned eighteen. As if it was some magical gateway, like I would go to bed on August 15th a boy and wake up the next day a man. I didn't of course, none of us do; and at nineteen I still feel like I did when I was fifteen.

I shower and try to not reopen the cut on my chin. I fail and have to sit on my bed dabbing it with toilet paper until I'm sure it has stopped and I won't bleed on my crisp white shirt. The shirt is a relic from college and the hospitality side of the course. Really this meant learning how to be a waiter in the restaurant the catering side of the course cooked for. Amongst my many useless talents I actually have it written down on paper that I know what wine goes in what glass, how to lay a table and how to serve people veg.

Have you ever been to a restaurant that has silver service? I haven't. Most of them dump your plate in front of you and run. Some of them will put a bowl of veg in the middle of the table and leave you to it, this is called family service. But I'm fully qualified in silver service so if you find a restaurant offering it give me a shout and I'll be sure to put my C.V in.

If you were to describe my hair, *mop* would probably be the first word that came to mind. Style would never feature unless it was pre-fixed with "no". I run a comb and then a brush through it and try and make myself presentable. It's too short for a band and a ponytail. Too long to just leave, in the end I try and slick it back hoping for Travolta in Pulp Fiction.

Mum says I look nice before adding it's a shame I don't have a jacket to go with the trousers. She doesn't ask where the trousers came from, she hasn't questioned any of the pairs that have appeared over the months but she must know. She hugs me, tells me to be brave and then tells me to hurry up. I obviously have no plans to drink at the wake, I mean I've knocked all that nonsense on the head but I walk into town. Just in case like.

Town only has one shop that sells men's clothing and I think it's ironic that trousers from work end up here. It's the kind of place where the staff immediately judge people as they enter. Any other day and I bet the old dude behind the counter would think I was off to court. He asks if he can help me and I say I need a black tie, all he does is nod in reply. He wanders off to the back of the store, comes back with one and asks if I can tie it myself. I say I used to wear one to school so I'll be fine.

He watches as I tie it, cringes as I hold it in my teeth and then smiles when I ask him how I look. He fixes my collar, adjusts the knot and tells me I look fine. I ask how much I owe him and he says there is no charge today. I ask him if he is sure. When I thank him he tells me not to mention it.

I'm late getting to Becky's place. She doesn't live with her parents anymore. She moved into a flat with her now ex-boyfriend and kicked him out when she caught him cheating on her. I'd like a place of my own but know I'd have to curb my spending habits. I keep telling myself when I have caught up with all the backlog of albums I don't own yet I'll start looking. Really I know I'll never own all the albums I want and it'll take being kicked out for me to sort my shit out, but until then I'll carry on as I am.

She looks stunning when she answers the door and I immediately feel scruffy. She's wearing a figure hugging black dress and heels so high she is almost as tall as me. You can see the church from her place so the walk only takes a few minutes. She loops her arm through mine and rests her head against me. I try not to smile or read anything into it, we are just friends going to another friend's funeral.

The church is already packed and we end up standing at the back. The rumours of speakers being outside prove to be true and there is easily another hundred or so people out there. I know it's wrong but I can't help wandering how many of these people would have turned up if it was me in the box at the front and not him.

We are half way through *How Great Thou Art* when Becky starts to cry. She doesn't make a sound as the tears pour. I put my arm around her and pull her in close, never wanting to let her go. She shrugs me off and fishes some tissues out of her handbag, composes herself and then holds my hand.

We stand like that for the rest of the service. It's all a bit of a blur. I'm more concerned with my hand getting sweaty or if anyone has noticed what's going on, than what the vicar is saying. I know at one point our old P.E teacher gets up and sings his praises and says how much he misses him. While he is speaking all I can think is how weird he looks out of a tracksuit.

After the service and out of the stale church air, people loiter around, unsure what to say or do next. I see my old college lecturer and we exchange a nod across the crowd. We didn't exactly part on good terms but today isn't about us. There is talk of taxi's and shared cars up to the cemetery and I suddenly regret not driving and being the hero of the day.

We share a taxi with Jane Ryder, who looks like she wants to say something to me but knows it's not the time or the place. Being the gentleman I am I pay and then we watch as our friend, someone we have known all of our lives is put into a hole in the ground. That's when it hits me that all of this is really real. That I'm really not going to see him again. I try to fight it. I really do. but when Becky squeezes my hand and tells me it's ok, the tears finally come.

The wake is at The Oak in town, it's a private affair for family and close friends. I respect them for that, they have lost their son, they shouldn't have to feed half the town as well. We all head for The Three Horseshoes, it isn't a planned destination it's almost an instinct.

The Shoes as it is known locally is where everyone our age drinks. It's where you drink when you're not really old enough and it's where you drink when you turn eighteen and want to see kids from the year below get asked for I.D. Jane is still tagging along and I ask her and Becky what they want. I fully intend on having a lemon and lime or maybe even an ice water but when I get to the bar I order a pint to go with the vodka and Cokes the girls are having.

I squeeze in next to Becky and we raise our glasses to him. From the first mouthful I know that this isn't going to be just a pint. It barely touches the sides and before the girls have even finished theirs, I am on my feet and asking if they are ready for round two.

This isn't me falling off the wagon, this is me jumping off it and running for the hills. The afternoon quickly falls into a drunken haze. People I haven't seen or thought about since school appear out of the woodwork and tell me I'm alright. Whatever that means.

Rounds are bought, drinks are spilled, punches are thrown, tears are shed. It is everything a wake in a small town should be and more.

It's gone six when Becky says she needs to go home to feed the cat and asks if I'll walk her home. Remembering the mistakes of my past I say I will. I almost make a joke about how it isn't raining but I don't want anything to spoil this chance, no matter how slim it is. We walk arm in arm through town getting dirty looks off shoppers and parents desperately trying to steer their children out of our way.

She talks incessantly all the way to her place about how it's been a lovely day and how it's what he would have wanted. I say that I'm sure he would have rather not died and she says I have a point. Back at her place I don't want to assume I am invited in and sort of stand awkwardly on the doorstep hedging my bets.

She reaches out, hold both of my hands and tells me to say something. This is it, this is the moment I have dreamed of for six years. I look straight into her eyes and tell her I love her. I tell her I have always loved her and I always will love her. In slow motion she lets go of my hands and pulls me to her.

Then we kiss.

It's not my first kiss but it may as well be. Nothing that has happened before is this magical. Nothing that will happen in the future will come close. Her tongue flicks into my mouth, her fingers run through my hair and then she pulls away. My heart crashes as I am sure she has realised who it is she is kissing. She looks at me, smiles and then sighs. One of those really content sighs not one born of disappointment.

She says we shouldn't do it like this, not the first time. We are better than a drunken fumble. I try to argue that it wouldn't be a drunken fumble but I know she is right. She tells me when the time is right, it'll be right, then tells me to go home and sleep it off.

Before I turn to go she kisses me on the cheek as if to reassure me. Every time I look back as I walk up the street she is still stood there on the doorstep watching me walk away. I give her a final look and a wave before I round the corner and then head straight for the off licence.

Carmen was in the year above me at school and has worked in the off licence for as long as I've been going in there. She greets me with a sarcastic *"long time no see."*

It has been a long time, I used to be a daily customer. She starts to tell me what's on offer, a habit we formed when I used to end up drinking whatever I could afford in the last few days before pay day. I tell her I want a bottle of vodka, she asks if I mean the cheap stuff or the really cheap stuff. For old time's sake I say the really cheap stuff and head home.

Mum isn't exactly shocked to see me drunk. She's seen me in worse states and really I think we both knew what was going to happen when I left the car at home. She asks how it went and I tell her he is really dead, that's it, he's in the ground. Game over.

I don't tell her about Becky. She asks if I've eaten and I'm suddenly aware I haven't had anything all day. I tell her I haven't and say I'll grab something after I've got changed. I trudge upstairs, sit on my bed, loosen my tie and open the bottle.

You always see the hero in films take a massive swig out of a bottle of booze before going and doing something courageous. They never flinch or gag, they rarely even get drunk. I take a massive gulp and as soon as the fluid hits the back of my throat I gag. It takes three attempts, but force it down because winners don't quit.

The second hit only takes two attempts to swallow, the third goes down in one. As does the fourth and fifth. I don't really remember the sixth and I assume there was a seventh and possibly even an eighth. The next thing I know Mum is rolling me onto my side and scooping sick out of my mouth.

Hendrix, Bonham, Scott, even the drummer of Spinal Tap died choking on vomit. I'm too young and nowhere near cool enough to die like this. Mum half carries, half drags me to the bathroom, dumps me in the shower and turns the water on.

It's freezing cold but she does her best to undress me and clean me up. Slowly but surely I start to sober up. That's when the tears come, back once they start they won't stop. Mum turns the shower off and wraps me in a towel. I guess I should be ashamed of the state I'm in but I lost any shame I had a long time ago.

I get to that point where I've almost stopped crying but there is just the occasional shoulder juddering sob. I start to apologise to her about being sick and being useless on the whole as she is drying me. She tells me to shush and lies me down on my side in my freshly made bed. She puts a bowl on the floor, tells me to lie on my side and says to get some sleep. I go out like a light. The blissful sleep of the drunk swallows me whole.

Mum is sat in the chair at the end of my bed when I wake up. It's still dark and my skull feels like it is three sizes too big for my head. She asks if I'm ok and I say I'll live. I ask if she has stayed with me all night but already know the answer, she looks shattered. I tell her to go and get some sleep and that I'll be fine. I go to the bathroom, there are still lumps of carrot in the plughole and the smell of vomit lingers in the air.

I go downstairs, grab a drink of water, force it down and then get all the cleaning stuff from under the sink. I scrub away until the sun starts to rise and when I'm done you could eat your dinner off the floor. I put all the cleaning stuff away and trying to drink more water.

Even though I've gone to work feeling worse I've already decided I'm going to ring in sick. Daryl really won't be happy but he can go fuck himself, not that I'll tell him that of course.

If she is up and about I might ask Mum to ring in for me. If she isn't I'll say I need the day off to look after her. Sometimes it worries me how easily lying comes to me. I tell myself that lying to people like him doesn't count. No one gets hurt by me throwing a sickie. The economy isn't going to collapse and we finish early on Fridays anyway.

Mum over sleeps so I use her as the excuse when I ring in. I can tell Daryl is pissed off with me but I haven't had a sick day in ages. Mondays used to be my go to sickie day. I'd go out on Sunday afternoon get drunk then wake up hungover on Monday. I used to ring in with stomach flu, regular flu, 24 hour bugs, 48 hour bugs, sickness, diarrhoea, sickness and diarrhoea. One time I just said I couldn't be bothered.

It took four Mondays in a row before they threatened giving me a warning. Six more before it actually happened. Unlike on the TV they couldn't just sack me, there are rules and procedures they have to follow. I walked away with a final written warning that stayed on my record for six months and that ran out the other week.

Daryl says I sound like shit when I speak to him. He isn't happy and there is an air of menace in his voice when he says he'll see me Monday. But really, what's he going to do? Work dealt with I do the only sensible thing and head back to bed.

Before I can get there Mum is up and really pissed about how late for work she is. Somehow she thinks this is my fault and that I should at least drive her in. I tell her I'm still going to be over the limit and go back to bed. I wake up hours later, somehow even more hungover than earlier. I shower and come out feeling almost human.

I put the telly on and flick through the channels. It's all chat shows, game shows and other boring crap. It's not even lunchtime and I'm already bored. Tom is still at school, everyone else is stuck at work. This is why I stopped throwing sickies.

There is only one thing for it, I've got to finish the tape. I've got like three hours until Tom gets out of school and only 45 minutes to fill so if I get a wriggle on I can totally pull this off. Plus I should totally be sober enough to drive by then.

Even though this is a rush job now I still blank over the start of side two, I still have standards to uphold. I then rewind the tape back to the beginning, take it out and run the spools forward with a pencil.

The best way to get a tape done fast is to go long. At a little over six and a half minutes long *Eraser (Denial: Realization)* off *Further Down the Spiral* is a brilliant way to start. It also captures my mood quite accurately. It's the sound of realisation after denial and my realisation is that I really shouldn't have drunk that vodka.

I don't think I was all that much in denial about my drinking. I mean I kind of had it under control. I just need to climb back on the wagon and carry on like I was and then not fall off it again.

I go even longer with the next track, *Scarecrow* by Ministry, it's over eight minutes long and still awesome. That's like quarter of an hour done without even thinking about it. Pitchshifter don't really have any really long songs so I go with *Triad*. It's another early, heavy one and another one I hope they wheel out come Tuesday.

I fancy a drink, that's the thing about alcohol it's a bit moreish. No matter how drunk I've ever gotten I've always gone back for more. There are a lot of spirits I can't drink anymore after over indulging on them, I refer to these as "sick drinks." Once you have tasted Bacardi backwards there is no going back to it. This is why vodka is so good.

I push aside the thought of getting drunk again and drop in *Super-Charger Heaven* by White Zombie. It's not very long really, but it sure is fast and one of those songs that begs to be played at an obscene volume. Given I've already filled half of the side with four songs I reckon I can afford to slow down a tad. Time wise like, tempo wise I don't think you can go too fast.

Remember that time I got punched in the balls crowdsurfing to Pantera? The time I left the queue to meet Max Cavalera? His new band Soulfly are really good, like really, really, good. Even though it has Fred Durst on it, *Bleed* hits the ground running and doesn't let up until it comes crashing to an end four minutes later. It's perfect for the tape.

I feel kind of bad hating on Fred Durst so much. I was a very vocal supporter of Limp Bizkit when they were first around. I got the store in town to order in *Three Dollar Bill Y'all$* for me before anyone else was even aware of them. I'm not saying I alone am responsible for their current colossal global fame but if you scale that down to this small, market town I totally am. The thing is once they were massively popular the shine kind of went off them. See I'd discovered Cold by then and no one had heard them.

It's not that I'm a musical snob or anything it's just that popular music tends to be awful.

A band you could never accuse of being popular are Will Haven, they supported Deftones last year and blew me away. If I had to describe what it is they do in one word, I'd probably say "noise." They are really intense, like super intense. I can barely get through their album in one sitting, it's that good. They are another band that I'd like Summer Holocaust to sound like. I'd never do it in front of anyone, especially Tom but when I'm on my own I try to sing like Grady Avenell. This one time I did it I screamed until I thought I was going to pass out, the time after that I threw up.

My go to tune of theirs is *I've Seen My Fate*, it's the second track on the album but the clear highlight for me. I cue the tape up, start recording and then spend the three minutes, forty seconds screaming my head off. Well most of the three minutes is spent coughing, heaving and trying not to be sick. Still forty seconds is way longer than I have ever managed before.

Next up I go for a song I know all the words to, *Down Rodeo*. Rage Against the Machine pretty much do what they say on the tin. I don't get all of the references but the anger translates well so that's what I focus on the most. While Will Haven screaming is hard, rapping just feels awkward. I'm sure if I keep trying I'll find a style that suits me and then we'll build Summer Holocaust around it.

I wonder if Becky can play an instrument? We don't really need backing vocals and if she sings then that's me out of the band. If she was willing to take lessons I'd totally buy her a bass. If she wanted to play drums I'd probably stretch to like paying for half of the kit. Drums are expensive. I thought I'd be a good drummer for a while but then we saw Fear Factory.

It's not natural what Raymond Herrera can do. I was utterly convinced he was backed up by a drum machine or a computer or maybe even another drummer but no it's all him. Sometimes when I see a band I come out ready to rock and get Summer Holocaust up and running. Other times I just don't see the point. Fear Factory are a case of the latter. Despite all this *Replica* is perfect for the tape.

I reckon *Replica* is enough to make even the best drummers out there want to cut their arms off. I can manage the opening riff but after that I can't keep up so stick to singing along with Burton C. Bell. At a smidge under four minutes long I've only got room for one more track and it's obviously got to be a Pitchshifter one.

W.Y.S.I.W.Y.G or *What You See Is What You Get*, is the obvious choice. It's off the new album and pretty much describes how I feel about myself at the minute. It's not so much that I hate myself. I mean I do, but I hate everything so it's not self destructive and that's alright isn't it?

After the girl across the road died and all the counselling, I tried to be positive. To see only the good in the world but it didn't work. We are all imperfect, all of us have our faults no matter how small. But some of us are more imperfect than others. I count myself amongst them obviously. My feet are too big and they are ugly as well. I'm either cripplingly self conscious or annoyingly arrogant and there is no middle ground. I over think some things but rush blindly into others and only realise I've messed up when it's too late to do anything about it.

After W.Y.S.I.W.Y.G finishes there is gap at the end of the tape, it's not quite a minute. Too long to leave, too short to fill with anything that really fits with the rest. It's almost brilliant but fails at the last minute. If this doesn't sum my life up I'm not sure what does.

When I first found out about the whole Straight Edge thing one band's name kept coming up, Minor Threat. They gave the scene its name after all. The only thing the record shop in town could find for me was their self titled album that combined two EP's, it was only available on tape and that felt right somehow. The entire album lasts seventeen minutes and all twelve of its songs fit on one side of the tape, they then repeat on the other side. The stereo in the car, like the one in my room has auto reverse and the album flashes by on a continual loop of unadulterated fury. It's a thing of utter beauty.

It pretty much lives in the car. It's perfect for the short trip to and from work. It gets me in the right frame of mind to face the day in the mornings and then vents the anger that has festered all day on the way home. If I had to get rid of every single piece of music I own apart from one, *Minor Threat* is the one I'd keep.

I already know they are going to bring the tape to a crashing end. It's now just a question of what track I can narrow it down to. I've still got an hour or so until Tom gets out for the day so I get the tape out of the car and listen to it twice before deciding that *Straight Edge* is the one.

I line the tapes up as best as I can and slot it in place. I'm a little rusty but it's a skill I'll never lose no matter how obsolete they try and make tapes. I rewind the tape and listen to *Straight Edge* again. By the time the deck reverses and Suck Mojo come back on I have decided I'm back on the wagon and never drinking again.

I draw a large X on my left hand with a black marker pen to prove this to myself. This is the mark of the Straight Edge, I've thought about getting it tattooed on my hand to make myself stick to it. I think a lot about tattoos, Dad always said not to get them even though he is covered with them.

What I think he means is don't get stupid ones, or drunk ones. He has his own name done on the inside of his bottom lip. He also has more breasts drawn on him than I have seen in my life. Like real ones, in the flesh, not porn ones, that would be silly.

I can't decide if I should pick Tom up from school and surprise him with the tape being finished or wait for him to come around later and then drop it on him. I toss a coin a few times until I get the answer I really want, grab the tape and leave the house.

I hated school, that's not exactly a surprise or a secret. But looking back I wish I had done things differently. Nothing that happens while you are at school really matters. The kids who bully you will be losers when they grow up. The kids who beat you at sport will end up playing Sunday league football and living off the story of how they had a trial for United before getting up Monday and going to the same type of shitty job you do. All that matters is you. If I could go back and give me any advice I'd tell me to stop worrying about all the crap that goes on and just look out for number one. That and to ask Becky out like.

I get to school a bit too early and am halfway through *Powertrip* when kids start to pour out. I've got the windows down and the stereo on as loud as it'll go. A few of them point and laugh but I ignore them. One little scrote comes over and asks if I can sell him any ganja. I ask him if I look like a drug dealer and tell him to piss off before he can answer.

Mr Robinson comes charging over and tells me to turn the music down. I briefly forget that I don't have to do what he tells me anymore and do it before asking him what he wants. He tells me I'm going to have to leave and ask him why. This stumps him but he says he doesn't want to call the police. We have a bit of a stand off before he mutters something under his breath and storms back.

Tom comes out before I get to find out if the police have been called or what crime I'm meant to have committed. He jumps in and I over rev the engine before spinning the wheels and rocket out of the car park. I turn the volume back up and yell that I have finished the tape. Tom looks pissed but I tell him it's all brilliant stuff. He asks what I've gone for and my mind blanks. I tell him it's a surprise but if he is up for it we can cruise round while he finds out. He says he needs to get changed, see his folks and grab something to eat but will be round later.

I drop him off at his place and head home. I take a bit of a convoluted route so I can listen to some more of the tape but it's not the same on your own . Mum is back by the time I get home. She looks exhausted and asks why I've got a cross drawn on my hand. I tell her I'm never drinking again and she gives me a look that says she doesn't believe me. I tell her how I'm going to get it tattooed on there and how this is it for life now. She rolls her eyes and tells me I need to take her to the supermarket. I tell her I can't as Tom is coming round in a bit and then we are going out. She tells me there isn't any food in the house and that she needs to go shopping.

I offer to give her a lift there and then the money to get a taxi back. I think this is a fair compromise, I mean I'm not a taxi service, if she wants to go places she can always learn to drive and buy her own bloody car. I don't tell her this of course, I'm not that stupid. She tells me she is tired and has had an awful day. I start to say that that isn't my fault before I realise that it really is my fault and ask her how long it'll take.

I wait in the car while she does the shopping. I'm parked by the doors facing an advert for New

Zealand lamb. If the poster wasn't behind a plastic screen I'd tear it down. I don't know what angers me the most - the disgusting consumerism or the image of the succulent chops.

Nine Inch Nails are on by the time she has finished and I'm in a foul mood. She asks me to turn the music down a bit as she has got a headache. I pretend I don't hear her. In the end she turns it down herself and I fight the urge to tell her to get the fuck out of the car. How dare she touch my stereo, in my car! Who does she think she is?

I begrudgingly help carry the bags into the house and dump them in the middle of the kitchen floor. She thanks me for taking her and asks if I want any tea. I'm starving I haven't eaten in days but the thought of food repulses me so I say I'm going to grab something with Tom later.

The world slides away from me as I'm going up to my room. I hold onto the banister until I can see straight again and tell myself I'm just dehydrated. In the bathroom I drink from the cold tap like some type of animal before splashing some water on my face. I'm not sure why I do this but it works in the movies.

It does actually seem to do the trick and feeling better I go and lay on my bed. I don't put any music on. I just lie there and stare at the ceiling, looking for patterns in the plaster. I must have dropped off at some point because the next thing I know Tom is punching me in the arm and telling me to wake up. I ask him what time it is and he says it's almost eight.

It's almost dark as we leave the house, the tape comes on halfway through *Triad* but I click stop and fast forward it to the end the second side. *Triad* being on the tape is no surprise, but I want Tom's first listen to be proper. Given we have ninety minutes to kill I do a few of the usual loops to the sonic accompaniment of first *Pigwalk* and then *Please Sir* before taking us out of town. I drive us aimlessly into the night, getting faster and faster as the music gets under my skin. We orbit town through lanes and housing estates before charging down the bypass. We're doing seventy, as fast as the hunk of junk has ever gone and Soulfly are doing their thing. The streetlights are sending the inside of the car orange in bursts as we dance in and out of their field. Tom's saying something but I can't quite hear him so I reach over and turn the music down.

My eyes are only off the road for a second, maybe two, tops, but when I look up we are almost at the roundabout. I stamp on the brakes, willing the car to slow down. Realising I'm not going to be able to stop in time I take my foot off the brake and yank the steering wheel round. I swear one of the back wheels must be off the floor as we screech our way round. It feels like we are going to tip over and then the back overtakes the front and we are pointing to where we have just come from.

I ask Tom if he is OK and it takes a while but he says he is. I start the car back up and take us back into town. Tom says how it was a good job there wasn't anyone else on the road and I say nothing. All I can think of is the funeral yesterday and Becky. I tell Tom I'm sorry, really sorry and it'll never happen again. I tell him I don't know what I was thinking, I tell him I wasn't thinking. He says it's fine and I think he means it.

I drop him back at his place and apologise again. He tells me to stop saying sorry. I pull off at a far more reasonable pace but don't go home. I circle town a few times, almost daring myself to go back to the bypass. I turn the music up a bit more, trying to make it take control like it did earlier. It doesn't work so I turn it up louder still.

I hurtle past the supermarket, it's closed now and the carpark is abandoned. I think about the lamb advert and how disgusting it is. How someone has to put it in the case so it can't be that hard to get it back out. I think about the manager's face when he opens up tomorrow and sees his capitalist gore-fest has been destroyed.

I turn the car around and pull into the car park. W.Y.S.I.W.Y.G is thundering out of the stereo as I walk over to the brightly lit advert. I can't see how the the case opens so I swing my fist into it. I've never been a fighter and I don't leave a mark even though it feels like my hand is going to explode.

I go back to the car and look for something to smash it with. I'm not going to be beaten, not this time, not tonight. Before I resort to the tyre iron in the boot I find yet another marker pen stolen from work. Minor Threat are screaming at me, I look at the X on my hand and know what I have to do.

In the best handwriting I can muster and the biggest letters that will fit across the screen I write "MEAT IS MURDER!" After all everyone likes The Smiths.

Made in the USA
Charleston, SC
06 September 2015